AF673927

# Boot Polish and Other Stories

Syed Afroz Ashrafi

HERITAGE

HERITAGE PUBLISHERS
NEW DELHI

Copyright © Heritage Publishers, 2011

All rights reserved. No part of this publication may be reproduced or transmitted in any form or by any means without the written permission of the publishers.

**HERITAGE PUBLISHERS**
19-A, Ansari Road, Daryaganj,
New Delhi - 110 002
Tel.: 23266258, 23264444
Fax.: 23263050
E-mail: heritage@nda.vsnl.net.in

ISBN: 978-81-7026-284-8

***Printed in India***
Sagar Printers, 23 Ansari Road,
New Delhi - 110 002

# Boot Polish and Other Stories

*Dedicated*

*to*

**Dr. Vandana Dutta**

*She left us rather prematurely to find abode in heaven.*
*Was a fine piece of work, a splendid creature indeed who lived*
*a very short life to leave us all shattered.*

## *Acknowledgements*

My first collection of short stories Silence of the Dead and Other Stories came about in the year 2007. Since then I have been into the making of the second collection of stories which have taken time that even myself would not have thought of. It did take the time unfortunately it was not supposed to. Primarily because writing stories has so much to do with finding the right flair and the human experience it rests on and secondly the lack of concentration for stories again demands the highest level of concentration I lacked terribly. But I must thank the forces and inspirations, the influences and impacts, the well wishers and the detractors for continually reminding me about the job that I ought to have finished long back but either it was my own unintentional procrastinations or the brewing dissension within the self or the rising skepticism of the unconvincing friends that hampered the progress of the soul and the artist. But in any case my thanks to all in the same measure because it is the belief that polishes off the tails of cynicism and induces the element of hope into a despairing situation.

A word of thanks must accrue to the likes of Dr. Quasim Khursheed, Dr. M. F. Helali, Dr. Saleh Ahmad Saif, Dr. Syed Mujeebuddin, Dr. Imteyaz Ahmad, Dr. Zamanat Abbas, Zia Abdul Wahab and Hemant Sharma for expressing faith in my creative talent and doing the necessary editing. Zia Abdul Wahab deserves a special mention for leisurely reading the manuscript and pruning the mawkishness of the texts. He took the long road and traveled carefully to avoid the semblance of any disorder about the stories.

He is indeed a friend and a younger brother held in the highest esteem. Dr. Shakibur Rehman Khan was a willing advisor who never doubted the book Boot Polish and other Stories being a reality. Dr. Rajkumar Sharma, a very intimate friend guided the stories to the logical routes with his razor sharp criticism and a healthy approbation of the stories. I must acknowledge his contributions.

Also, I would be unfair if I do not recall the unexpressed wishes of some of the best individuals under this sun who genuinely believed that I can write fiction and in the best of times and the worst of periods they threw their weight around and took me to the safer waters unscathed. My heartfelt thanks to them. My father Prof. Wahab Ashrafi, a critic of Urdu literature knew that the inheritance would continue and this book is an extension of the same intellectual tradition. He coerced me into a faith being honoured by this book. The book Boot Polish and Other stories is finally in your hand and as a writer of the stories I cannot feel comfortable unless it is generally regarded by the readers as something readable. I am waiting to hear from you soon.

***Syed Afroz Ashrafi***
ashrafiafroz@gmail.com

## *Contents*

# Vestibule

The shadows refused to emerge, the long trees studded with leaves fluttered in frenzy, the mild summer stood hapless to beam heat, the subdued sun signalled its inability to unleash the fire it relishes and the afternoon seemed clad in a friendly mood as if it is going for reconciliation with those it had tormented in the recent past.

The wide courtyard stood barren bereft of the song and dance it had been a witness to recently. It was a dull afternoon and all seemed resigned to the comfort of the room. Amma sat in the verandah, talking to herself rolling her fingers on the beetle with catechu spread across it. It was very strange to see her doing it alone and engaged in a conversation with the self. Only recently she had developed this rather strange habit or may be for she thought her daughter existed in her imagination. It was the period of lull in her life, a period that made her think about her lonely self after the exit of her daughter, Sheelu. Sheelu had gone only six months ago wedded to an engineer in Gwalior and since then it sapped all her vitality. Shahzaad, her son was a very private person, the maid Hamida normally interfered with the silence with her bulk and the sounds of the footsteps. She was there with Amma as her surrogate companion, her lieutenant, her close aide but still somewhere she thought she was not in her elements. Mamujaan had also left just the other day and the afternoons that used to engage the two looked back only to be reminded that no longer the voices are there, of the two, of the intimate sounds of chuckles, of the tales drawn from the locale of the childhood, from the days of the murky past, from the periods of the history and from the selective moments of some reverberating days. Shahzaad noticed all these, could sense the relative quietness, the unrest within Amma but he could barely say anything. He was not the kind who would share the grief within a body or can have words that can heal the invisible wounds for he knew Sheelu will not come back to be with her, to be the same ebullient girl as now she was the wife of somebody tied by the mores of the social compulsions, wedded to the responsibilities induced by the sense of belonging to a different milieu. He too was not the fellow who goes round the house and keeps all engaged to distract the concentration from the broken memories Amma was desperately clinging to.

His father had deserted him very early on and he had just a faint memory that helps him build a portrait of him but beyond it it's all mist. The evening was cool, the breeze gently caressed the ears, the moon peeped through the patches of clouds and the streak of golden light fell on the floor as if it was going to be a night with some stars falling on the ground and those around are waiting to catch them. Sheelu, thought Shahzaad, would normally during the summer evening do all necessary things to make it the conference room, the discussion forum, the centre of all attention as women from neighbourhood would come and engage Amma for all kinds of talks while he would drop in and out to see the women folk engaged in myriad talks ranging from weather to wither and wild forays at times without coherence, at times without the nods of the many around but there was one common agreement that the courtyard impressed all. Rafiqan, Mehrun, Chanda, Nafisan, Haleema and the talkative Qamrun regaling them with tales picked up from all houses as whose daughter in law had abused mother in law and as to whose daughter is using thick lipstick and whose sons are worthless fellows only chasing damsels. One of the stories that Shahzaad still remembers and is firmly entrenched in his mind, was that of the Tahmina's daughter as how she duped her own mother in the mid of afternoon and went away with Salim Sheikh to be retraced from the orchard of Khalid Mahmood. She was good at adding spices to the tales and he still remembers her words "see Tahmina acts very innocent and what she said to defend her daughter, followed by a pause, she would regain her flair." Roxana only wanted to talk to Khalid Mahmood regarding the advances of his son and you know both of them were chided by him only. And then in a much muffled tone she would whisper, what a boy will do with a girl when nobody is around and then she would gaze at faces to see the reactions of the women around her. Shahzaad's mother would often advise her not to churn out tales and outrage somebody's modesty to which she would in her inimitable style say, na, Bibi, na, Allah Qasam, I do not want to damage anybody but it is a fact. Tales generally mired in fiction was the recipe she often produced with natural flair. Haleeman took some special interest in her tales since she had sons only and she thought she had nothing to fear. While all these went on, Sheelu would sit in the verandah with Hameeda waiting to receive orders from Amma for the hospitality. Shahzaad disliked these women, almost hated them for their tendencies and the habit of intruding into the privacy of the houses.

Khamispur was a small village with about two hundred houses, has a long history of growth. It came about as the final pocket of the Muslims in the aftermath of the widespread communal riots and those who could not move away to Pakistan settled there and turned it into their dreamland. The village had all the ingredients of what constitutes a village, the paddy, the long stretches of unused land, the houses some still wearing the old look of the kutccha mud walls raised through thick bamboo sticks and straws with wooden pole at the centre of the roof to provide the necessary support. Those days' houses were like hamlets scattered around a wide area and the open field around it reigned in fresh air to ward off the blues of summer. Maulvi Ahmad Hameed was the first of the refugees to settle down and he had a pivotal role in building the whole village. He was uprooted from his native place Amirabaad and had to flee from there as the riots broke out. Left home and hearth and with a group of people he discovered the place called Khamispur which today is a densely populated village. This is why most of the Galis and Chowks are named after him and the surviving members of his family though moved away some time later in pursuit of bread though they have remained connected to the land by paying occasional visits. Shazaad's father was also one of the uprooted men who sought refuge in the same village and Shahzaad often finds Amma talking about the ruins and the reconstruction. Amma was still obsessed with the idea that Khamispur was responsible for the premature death of her husband. He came over there only to be plagued by a series of problems and one of the major epidemics that broke out consumed his life. Though Shahzaad was raised in the same village, much of his childhood was spent under the greenwood trees of the same village; he could not strike an emotional response with it. May be for he thought the village killed his father since the medical attention that ought to have been available to him, was not there. Moin Chacha was very close to his father and most of the stories of the yesteryears, he got from him only. It was very normal for Moin Chacha to offer fajr prayer and look for the houses where he can find the morning tea and since Shahzaad was very close to him he came directly from the mosque to his house. Amma did not like him at all for she thinks that it was Moin only who brought her husband to Khamispur and therefore had an indirect role in his death but Shahzaad leaves it to the will of God.

That morning he was sitting on the verandah of his house waiting for tea with the newspaper in his hand and while calling Amma for the tea, he saw Moin Chacha making his way to him. It was a common sight for the people of Khamispur to see Moin loitering around, sticking to the houses wherever he could find space. Some of the elderly members of the village knew him very well like Quddus Khan, Abbas Jilani, Qadeer Islam, Kaleem Heyat and Shiv Shankar Nath. Moin Chacha had become a household name and the women were really wary of him. He had lost his wife long way back but had two sons. Both were married and lived in the same village but the daughters-in-law did not care for him. It was quite a habit with Moin Chacha to find cups of tea at the expense of some vituperative words for his sons and daughters-in-laws and the story had gained currency that Moin was almost like an orphan discarded by his own sons. Shahzaad's father had left behind some land and Maulvi Hameed had established a school in the village using his pre-partition political connections that introduced education in that village and Shahzaad did study there until matriculation and then moved to the city to complete his education. Today he is a government officer posted in a block not too far from the village and he and Sheelu are the lifelines of Amma.

Sheelu was growing up and Amma had her own concern for her since it was a general practice to put daughters to marriage early on but Shahzaad did his bit in delaying her marriage for he wanted her to have moderate education. Sheelu was tall, hazel eyes, the construction of face reminded of round moon, the nose finely crafted, the complexion oozed light and radiance. Amma was growing old and Sheelu gradually took on the mantle of the domestic responsibility. Aslam Farooque, known widely as Mamujaan, had found a suitable match for Sheelu. But Sheelu was not in the right frame of mind to accept the decision that was about to be taken. The next day Qadeer Islam, Quddus Khan, Hakim Ashraf all were squatting on the verandah to discuss the issue since Aslam Farooque had invited them over a cup of tea. Amma did not seem very keen to have any kind of discussion about Sheelu as she could see the strain on her face and she knew further that Sheelu is not the kind of girl who would ever say anything to anyone whether she likes it or not. Aslam Farooq was waiting for Moin Chacha and asked Shahzaad to look for him though it was only customary since Moin Chacha had comical value and all agreed that Moin should be there and to get his opinion was equally important. Shahzaad went round the village looking for Moin Chacha and he found him taking long strides forward inching towards his house. He held on there and came back with him. Inside the house the women like Rafiqan, Haleema and Musthari were busy with the kitchen works.

It seemed to be a festive occasion; the sense of something important being done permeated the atmosphere. Amma and Sheelu were very quiet; Shahzaad though appeared involved too did not have his heart into it. Mamujaan was the only one excited and he disclosed the family where Sheelu was to be in matrimonial alliance. As soon he disclosed the name of Altaf Kapdawala, all eyes went searching fraught with a sense of astonishment for they knew he was a big businessman of Hameedpur, had made a good fortune but very little was known about his ancestral history. Moin Chacha's lips opened up but as soon as he looked into the eyes of Mamujaan, his lips hung in air and he had to close it down. A moments silence made its way; Shahzaad stood up and darted inside the house to check Amma. Mamujaan continued his rhetoric. See marriages are made in heaven and we have no choice in the matter and I know all of you might think about his past or the background or the kind of history but opulence has no religion and poverty checks the quality of bones. Sheelu will be very happy for the family she is going into and she would be living like a princess. Do you know, Mamujaan went on, Altaf Kapdawala has many textile mills, does export of the garments and he has one son and a daughter only? Amid all these Hameeda emerged with cups of tea that broke the chain of Mamujaan's rant. Moin Chacha picked up the cup, took the cigarette thus far tucked between fingers, lighted it and took a long puff of disapproval. Rest of the people did not have too many words and they only gazed and gesticulated in uncomfortable ways. Finally it was decided that the issue did not call for more deliberations and Mamujaan stamped the seal of approval to his own proposal without waiting for the nods from those who were supposed to advise.

Amma walked inside the house, the frequency of beetle picked up rage while Sheelu was a model of compliance. She was lost to her own self, without language and the emotions dried up under the weight of Mamujaan's authority. Shahzaad took Amma to one of the rooms, held her hand, looked into her eyes and found her a portrait in endurance. Shahzaad knew that she is not happy, not at all for Sheelu was her life, her soul and just about everything. Tell Amma, you do not have to bother much about Mamujaan for he does not know what it means to get a daughter married off since he himself has remained a bachelor. As Shahzaad was speaking to his mother, Amma, he felt a new kind of energy erupted within her. She spitted the remains of beetle, stood up and came out in the courtyard and ordered all women to leave since the feast is over and expressed her thanks to them. She called on Mamujaan who just had taken off his sherwani, ensconced comfortably on the sofa, smoke puffed up his face, the dark complexion seemed even darker under the spell of smoke, was surprised to see his sister cantering in his room with confident steps. Shahzaad fell behind Amma and held on at the doorstep. Mamujaan thought that his sister has come to thank him for the proposal has been finalized. Amma sat very close to her brother and banged a question that pushed her brother to the edge of his seat. Bhai Saab, Sheelu is my daughter and I have not given the right to determine her future to anybody and any decision regarding her marriage cannot be final unless I approve it. Mamujaan was left in shreds; he regrouped himself and addressed her as Khalida, her name, what is wrong with you. You are questioning my decision, my decision, he repeated it. Yes. I question it strongly. Retorted Amma with whatever ferocity she could develop. Mamujaan, fumed, fumbled and fretted. Shahzaad and Sheelu peeped through the curtain to see their audacious mother, the Amma, a different Amma who had rediscovered her aggression after years of regression. Shahzaad, held Sheelu's hand, sheelu acknowledged the emotion of her brother by looking into his eyes. Both brother and sister were more than gay to see their Amma asserting herself and downsizing the inflated stature of Mamujaan who had been wielding enormous influence on the family, on everybody and even on the village of Khamispur.

Amma stood up from the sofa and asked Mamujaan either to mend his ways or leave as early as possible for the future of her kids is something to be decided by her only. Mamujaan's cigarette fell on the ground, hands were trembling, legs shuddered, the rage disappeared, the anger he was so friendly with deserted him and he found himself stripped of all power, all might and all awe in a matter of minutes. Amma came out with long powerful strides, kissed the forehead of Sheelu, held Shahzaad's hand and hugged them hard as if the two are the inseparable parts of the body. Mamujaan stood his ground for a while, put the sherwani on, the cap of arrogance had lost its sheen and legs that walked in anguish produced muffled sounds of resignation. Amma, called Hameeda in a tossed up voice and asked her to call Moin Chacha all at once. Hameeda almost ran and in no time she was back with him. Moin, Amma, thundered, you must check with Khalid Mahmood today only. Moin Chacha could barely say anything other than looking into Amma's eyes. And finally he assured her not to worry for he will get things sorted out soon. But soon he asked Hameeda to bring a cup of tea for him and some snacks if possible and took a chair very close to Amma as if he was asking how you rediscovered yourself? Moin Chacha it was told to the two kids later on was supposed to marry Amma but somehow the things did not fall in place since Amma's father was not prone to the idea of handing over his daughter to somebody like Moin who took life as nothing more than a sport but Amma liked him or was there something more to it?

# Untouchable Anshu

She did not look back, not the least and the insistent strides thrust the pace she herself did not know how to arrest. What was that, why the urgency held her so badly, why the seeming hate did not have the kind of explanation, she in the normal course would have loved to question? The sky above the head seemed engrossed in heaping a bluish light on the earth and the light that fell sufficed perhaps to convince Anshu that she can walk the pace she wanted. Life has been a burden, quite a burden, her every moment was a burden, quite a burden on her short statured self. Stricken at times by the shard of nostalgia, at times by the day light that crept into her room through the iron rods of her window, her mother's quiet self, her father's round face, enveloped in quietude, the tongue hardly rolled ever and her little sister, Anni, and her doll, her delightful childhood and her own growing adolescence, her growing nipples, breasts assuming forms and with it went the physical sensation of being young, being responsive to the newly born desires. But her mother never had a kind word for her, never had the look of satisfaction and perhaps she never trusted her for she thought her just a girl with no commonsense or if at all it was there it never made its appearance to the outside world. Bewildered by the unsavoury turn of events early on in life pushed her to the brink of an unmanageable loneliness and she while being up against the walls of the boarding school where she had spent most of her days, good or bad, exciting or dull, in the midst of nuns, fathers and the typical Christian environs where things were spoken in hushed up tones, howls were lost in the maze of darkness and the cries lurched mostly inside the chest. Her father was not hers, a tall but square constitution, his eyes never rested on her but on the parts she thought she would fiddle with and the eye contact was never there. He was mostly traveling to the far end of the world and her mother sometimes went with him. He was a quiet man with not many words, spoke once in a while. A mother's friend, a close friend, a childhood friend who waited for her to be divorced, to be freed from the confines of parental absolutism, that forced her into a marriage with Agarwals. She did not protest and willingly tied the nuptial knot. Six months later she ran away while her former husband was in the States. By then, she was carrying the child, a pregnant woman, had to deliver that child much to her own chagrin. That was Anshu, me, the unfortunate child born under the duress of conjugal compulsions and that was the moment perhaps I turned into an object of hatred. Her husband, one did not file any case in the court for my custody and I was left to the lap of my grandmother who herself lived a very short life after the intrusion of a child thrust into her lap. My days in her lap had seen the early flutters of life, the songs were sung by the staggering voice of the grandma and I was negotiating the profound uncertainties of life.

I toddled on my knees, growing with a sense of burden and every day that passed by shortened my life by a day the feel of a human body in flesh and soul and I smiled back. My grandfather in whose lap I carried myself forward into the intricacies of the mundane existence, whose hands caressed the child thrown at the mercy of the church wardens, whose body was a shade against the blazing sun, whose lips I touched to get whenever he wore a half, hesitant smile. Learning the tricks of the trade by clinging to a flickering finger of the lurking life of an old man waiting to be consumed by the lingering shadows of gloom. Gloom was an inseparable part of my life, I never objected to it, rather kept it clung to my bare chest as the final gift of a mother who was more than relieved to almost abandon a child delivered from a reluctant womb. My grandparents left in no time, one after another and perhaps that was the moment I lost whatever protection I had. Left to the mercy of the indifferent stars, to the glorious uncertainties ahead and to the dramatic oscillation in the life of a child abused by nature and cursed by the human heart. My mother turned towards me hesitantly after the exit of my grandparents though she never had the desire to do it. She returned from Costa Rica after almost six months to see the fate of a suffering child waiting to be lifted by her own mother but her steps were coy, hesitant and she found herself under a social obligation, the ways of the world goaded her into realizing the ominous responsibility of raising a tear laden, grief-stricken, lightless, numbed and paraplegic burden to guide it to a direction. It was finally decided to put me to the confines of the boarding school. My mother along with her husband came to the town in a huff, to the house, to the same bleak house where I spent my claustrophobic days in the absence of all conceivable lights. I turned twelve, the year my grandparents left without entertaining any thought about my future that was so entirely uncertain, so completely bereft of the very shadow which could have accepted me in its own lap. I rejected all thoughts of being taken care of, drifting in and out of life, breathing in and out at the prospect of another exile in the form of a boarding school. My Mausi, a divorcee aged thirty-five wanted to adopt me and she thought her sister would readily accept her offer but my mother had a callous contempt for me, she knew the offer but chided her into silence. I was again bleeding but I had no defense against it. My mother's husband was rather stupid in the sense that he never looked at me and never spared a word of sympathy for after all I was the daughter of his rival who had lost his love due to him at least for a short while. His point of view I could comprehend even at that tender age. The same night while I lay in my bed alone, watching the movement of the fan that a voice drifted out of his room, and he was heard speaking to his wife. Do it fast, whatever you have to about this dirt to which my mother could barely say, yes in a day's time. I was more than certain that I have to fend for myself and see this life going to shreds. The next day, the three of us started for Darjeeling, my next destination where I was going to be dumped, where I would be raising myself through the support of the surrogate guardians, where the life would be humming the disconcerting songs, the troubled saga of a life lived under the shadows of loneliness but who cares. My fellow passengers were mum throughout though occasionally they murmured something incoherent, I looked or rather stole some looks at them while they were looking the other way. I was twelve only and the adolescence was creeping up a bit as I could notice the physical changes occurring to my body. Just a few days back I had found myself bleeding between the legs and that had terrified me completely. I cried out of ignorance, out of pain and out of horror. My Mausi, very quickly told me all about the complexities of a growing girl and I could believe this only after she told me with evidence that it has happened to her and this is something so natural that happens to all growing girls.

I was hungry almost famished and waiting for something to be taken as dinner. The train was running at a furious pace, the long barren stretches of darkness being negotiated with ease, I peered through the window to see the situation outside. It was pitch dark, wide stretches of land with lots of greenery I could see in the light reflected through the glass panes of the AC window. My stomach was burning and I was trying to divert the attention. In AC-2, compartment I was sitting on the lower berth while the upper one was to be that of mother's husband. Hunger was piled on hunger and I thought if my Mausi were around and if I had uttered anything like hunger she would have laid the table with things I could not have imagined but my own mother was so disinclined to see the muffled sounds of hunger forming holes in the stomach of her own daughter. But was I her daughter, a point I did not realize. Soon the waiters who were moving about the corridors of the compartment, carried trays of food looking for the berth number they noted while receiving orders. I did not know when they exactly ordered for things. Maybe while I was away to the toilet. I evaded all such thoughts as how and when they ordered and stayed focused on what was served to me in that tray brought by the waiter. I hurriedly tore the wrapper. A strong aroma of chicken curry hit my nostrils, plus salad, pickle and two breads apart from a handful of rice. I thought, though it is not enough to quell my hunger but still it can reduce the intensity. I did not wait, did not bother what the unholy couple was doing. I pounced on the food and took some hefty crumbs and gulped it down as if a waiting beggar outside the temple. I could feel I was under the surveillance of the roving eyes that rested on me every now and then but I was careless much the way my own mother has been. After I finished the food I felt some life creeping back into my body. I stretched my folded legs that almost touched the feet of my mother and she pulled it back. The untouchable child touching her feet was not acceptable to her. Her husband scanned the magazine in his hand with glasses on that seemed to be resting on his nose breaches. Sometimes he would pull it down and look around and again push that up. Perhaps the journey was a burden for him and he wanted to run through it quickly. I heard him saying, train kills and you forced me into it. We could have taken her ticket too or else your sister could have joined her here and we could take the plane.

My mother seemed to be nodding her head and said in a very low voice, that alternative is gone and you have to face the pain the journey of train entails. He kept quiet and looked at me with utter contempt. I was such a dirt for him. He had his own reasons to dislike or hate me but to see my mother's agreement was something incredible. Whatever I have known her in all these years, I could say with a measure of confidence that she has been a mother without the emotional complexities of a mother. Though that is not the case with my half sister, Anni who is loved and taken care. In fact she was left with the Au pair in Chennai and what I thought that maybe my mother did not want me to have any interface with her or maybe she wanted to keep her away from me since I was the condemned, circumstantial child who deserved to be alone and castigated for her unfortunate birth.

With all these I went to the bed. The berth was fairly comfortable, pretty wide, the bedroll good enough for the comfort and the pillow under head soft to welcome the onrushing sleep. I put my head on it and closed eyes as if I was interested in the things around. The couple shrunk and almost bumped into each other like a roll of clothes. I ignored it and put myself to the jerks of life along with the jerks of the running train. I drifted to sleep in no time and did not know what the couple did for the rest of the night. I must confess, the moment I closed my eyes, the face of my Mausi appeared before me, in torrents of tears, a numbed face without its normal gloss and the anxious, tense heart, skipping heartbeat to send off somebody whose sobs were hers, whose vision she shared and whose troubles she considered her own. My surrogate mother had whispered into my ears right at the point of departure "I will come to see you and be fair to your mother." I wondered whether my conduct as a daughter of an estranged mother left anything to be desired.

The formalities of admission were completed and I was handed over to the aliens, to the house I never thought was mine, to a place I had no sense of identity with; to the people I did not know. A child of twelve years was asked to live her own life with her fading energy. I was dismayed to see my mother leaving me with just one word. Don't do anything silly. This is your final opportunity. I did not understand what exactly she meant by final opportunity and the word silly. Still I thought she must have said something sensible. They left the same evening by flight which must have comforted her husband. I came back to my room where three girls already had their beds well placed to the different corners and mine was the fourth one, very close to the window and it opened out in the backwaters of the school. Sherwood Society as it was called, ran and managed by the Christian diocese. The British design of the building, the curved and hanging structure, the oval shaped boundaries, the hugely erected walls and the long trees encircling it reminded me of a prison house, where I was caged and was told to be there as the inseparable part of my existence. The three girls came from different backgrounds. I quickly learnt and struck a rapport with them. They were Amisha, Celina and Rabia. Myself Anshu, Anshu Patel from Gujarat while they were from Bombay, Madras and Moradabaad. The next day was school though the session had already commenced two months back and I was all the more confused as from where I have to start but much of my tension was eased through the willing support of the three inmates who kept me guiding and supporting. One of the things that really ailed me was the phone calls they received every second third day from their homes. And then they will come back to the room happy and jocund and spill tales of homes, people, brothers and sisters and all minor details. I was silent and they watched me keeping low, morose and lost. They questioned me too often, even wanted to know what exactly ails me but most of the times I would parry the question and push them to an academic question and they would lose the concentration. But deep down I was sick, really sick not to find anybody asking my well-being, keeping no tab on whatever I was doing there. This was a freedom to launch myself into a world that did not stop me from going wild. The first three months quickly passed and the involvement with the syllabus did not give me the space to think. If at all I thought of anybody, it was my Mausi, whom I missed and missed badly. I wanted to find some connections with her but my mother had left an instruction to the warden that in the event of any emergency they can contact the given numbers and when I checked the numbers, it were all overseas. I thought how careless and mindless my mother might have been while leaving overseas numbers of contact. I then decided to write a letter to my Mausi and give her the address of the school and the guidelines for the place if at all ever she desired to come here. But I thought it might be an offence to my mother as why she did not make her my local guardian while she has been away from the country. I was confused and thought to consult my friends but the danger was to tell them the secrets of my life, the indifference of my mother, and the details of her husband. I decided otherwise and in the process prolonged my own punishment.

I received no communication from my mother in the last three months and this was something I could not understand as how a parent can be so unconcerned about her own daughter. This perhaps, I thought was the punishment doled out to me for being the unwanted child, for being the deterrent to her life, for being a burden she always wanted to be divested of and I remained the solitary reaper, humming my songs of despair and destitution without letting it know to anybody who could have shared my loneliness, my fortitude, my pains and my disgust but I was learning to walk the tight rope, the abandoned streets of life, the darkness ridden holes but I was not terrified for I knew the way up to the life is going to be just that. My friends were eagerly awaiting the first semester break and they had their plans well made. All three of them seemed ready to execute their plans with precision, with excitement and with zeal. I had nothing to plan, nowhere to go, and nothing at all which could induce some excitement into my monotonous life. I thought of Mausi, she was the one who would really wait for me, the one who cares and brooks my tantrums, but I did not know how to contact her and ask her to talk to the administration of the school to let me go to her. All these had pushed me in a quandary, in a shell that incapacitated me for all practical purposes. I thought when all my friends left and the school closed down for the break, I would be the only one patrolling the walls and the boundaries of the school, that horrified me but I had no option. I stood resigned and yelling at my fate. In the last three months I had developed some associations with the boys of the school, of my own class and some of them seemed very inclined towards me. Ravish was the one with whom I walked some steps on the campus of the school, to the cafeteria and to the backwaters though meeting with boys outside the school was not permissible. His eyes fascinated me, very slim, tall legs that moved swiftly and what eyes my God. I nearly sank into them. His eyes were sparkling, produced the magical spell and honestly I was very conscious to avoid eye contact because when mine met his, I felt transported. He did not know anything about my feelings, though he lunged towards me at the slightest pretext and I was more than happy. I formed images, adored them and discarded them.

Only yesterday I was standing alone about the corridors of the classroom that he happened to be there and came running to me, Anshu, Anshu, and I pretended to take no notice of his calls. He thought I am not listening but again that left me restless and ran towards him as if I wanted to hug him, to go round him and take him into my arms to be put on the flight of fancy, to escape the dilemma of being, to ward off the challenges of being alone but all my fancies were brought to a sudden halt by the shout of sister Imalda, who asked me to get back to the classroom. She was the campus administrator and she used to rummage through the whole campus keeping vigilance on the activities of the students. Gradually the days inched closer to the break and there was excitement in the air all around and everybody seemed delighted to have a break from the pangs of the boarding school. Again I was thoughtless about the onrushing semester break and there only I thought of Ravish. Perhaps he too would be going to his parents. The same day I and he walked together to the cafeteria and on way to it I banged the question on him. Ravish, where you would be going this semester break. He was not prepared for this question at all that I could guess from his expressions. He thought a bit, "I have not decided, may be, to my Aunt who is in Chennai" but I interrupted, "not to the parents." For a moment I thought, there is one more like me in this world but soon dismayed to find that his parents are in States and they would be coming during the next Semester break only and that is six months away. You, his question left me speechless and in a fix as to how to find an answer that will be a reasonable one. I somehow could tell that my problem is very much like him that is my parents too were overseas. Then, you would be sulking here only. May be, just may be. Ravish, ran wild "ok, wonderful, we can be together here during the break and maybe I write to my Aunt in Chennai that I am staying on here because my friend Anshu is here. Come on, I am not in the mood to comprehend your jokes. It is not a joke, it is just possible, and at least we will have the company." I felt like going mad and prayed to my formless God to make it really happen. To be with him, talking to him, looking into his fizzy eyes, would be the real pleasure. The sensation ran down my body and I took some long strides forward to the surprise of Ravish, who literally had to run to keep pace with me. "Oh, oai, Anshu, what's wrong, why are you running baby." It sounded very pleasing to be addressed as baby from somebody you think you like him. At twelve to be addressed as baby has its own thrill. I looked towards him with all persuasion in eyes that perhaps Ravish could get but I was not sure for his expressionless face left no message and he went back, leaving me there for he had to do his works for the next day. I felt like crying but could not say, "please Ravish, be with me for some more time." This has been a problem with all growing girls that if they feel something good about somebody they will take hundred thousand years in acknowledging it. I had the same problem but still I was too wary of Ravish's reactions to whatever I might be saying to him and I had the fear also that I just may lose him even as a friend if I disclose my feelings to him. That was that. I came back to my room as if I had the opportunity to say something to somebody and I failed again to do that. I was upset with myself for not being able to have the gusto to tell something. I condemned my own inability to do it.

Sister Imalda took some long steps forward and her walk was always fearful for she had some news to break and I found her coming towards me since I was just outside my room. "Hi, Anshu, there is a call for you." Mine, I was almost bewildered as in the last three months calls were dreams for me and was there anybody in this world who had had the leisure to call Anshu and I said no, she might be mistaken but I still found her insistent and started walking with her. She talked very little, perhaps short of words or words did not come to her whenever she moved her lips to say something. Whose call it is, I asked hesitantly and there was a quick response for a change, from Chennai. I was immediately reminded of my dear Mausi. It must be she; I thought and geared myself up for an interface with her. Thoughts appeared like leaves and the short distance from my room to the warden's office appeared miles to me and in the process of all these thoughts I outpaced Sister Imalda who fell behind me. She kept coming in her usual strides and I darted inside the Warden's office, only to be told to wait by Sister Licia. I stood still, waiting for the ring to blare. My heart was not with me, beating at a good pace and the ring went, I pounced on receiver only to find my dear, dear Maussi on line. Hi, Anshu, this is Mausi, Mausi and my voice went numbed, choked my throat, speechless for a while, and my Mausi kept blaring "Anshu, Anshu, I am coming, I am coming dear. How are you my child," and I regrouped myself to answer her queries. "Hello Mausi, How could I be, what do you think I am very happy here, very comfortable and where you were in the last three months? You behaved like your own sister." I lodged all protest in a single go and Mausi, on the other end replied all my queries with her profound tears. "My child, I will tell you all when I come to pick you up for the vacation. Take care, my child, I will be there soon." I hung up the phone and stayed rooted to the ground for a while, to which Sister Licia did ask,"all is ok dear?" I nodded my head and walked away from there, engaged in a flurry of thoughts. I threw myself to the bed in a fit of rage for the call was a storm in the hopeless life of a girl, learning to be alone in this world. It also spoiled my plans to be with Ravish during the break. It was my fancy but somehow I thought, it could have some elements of reality. But still what was really tormenting me as how Mausi, got the numbers of the school and how my mother allowed her to act as a surrogate guardian and come and take me away for the vacation. This was something very thoughtful for me as I knew my mother best and under no circumstances she could have allowed me to be with Mausi during the break for she did not like me being so attached to her. I wanted to ask it but Mausi hung up the phone since she said she is coming and she would tell all.

The following day Ravish sat close to me just outside the cafeteria, holding his coffee in his right hand and the left one, perhaps, perhaps touching my own hand hanging loosely. I watched all these and wanted to know whether it was deliberate or just a chance but he seemed to be doing it and looked into my bare eyes. I thought he wanted to say something, something I was waiting for but he did not say even a word. Stood up and asked me to come with him. Puzzled, I stood up and started walking behind. A little away from the cafeteria he held my hand, held it firmly and as firmly as possible, I made no effort to be freed from the maiden sensation of the hand being held by somebody I always wanted him to hold it. He still was silent, but the hands kept brushing mine, his eyes ran down frantically on my whole being, and then Anshu, I know all about you, he shot a sentence that left me surprised. What do you know about me? There was a silence that stood between us, for a short while, but he himself started again, "I know you are a wonderful girl; a really magical girl who can inspire a dull heart and make it beat again. You are a splendid girl, Anshu, whose eyes can fill the eyes of the world with a rare vision, with the golden light, with a mysterious dimension just about everything." His rhetoric went on and every single word was like a salvation for me. I felt salvaged. He turned around, looked into my vacant eyes and in no time his lips rested on mine, then, he put his lips firmly on mine, holding me close to his heartbeat and I made no effort either to disapprove of it or to say anything to acknowledge it but one thing was sure, I was kissed by the man I wanted to be kissed. He himself blushed more than I did and I had no regrets. It was a maiden brush with a boy. Ravish left without a word, this was an expression of my feelings and I meant it. He left immediately without looking back and I fell behind him. I gradually strode back to my room with all my properties intact. I came back to my room, resigned myself to the waiting bed and closed my eyes. My lips were still wet, the fleck of his saliva stayed inside my mouth, the wonder of a kiss, the magic of a kiss, the power of kiss all was with me and there I realized my own feminine power. I did not wash my mouth for some hours until it was compulsory. I retained the much savored male saliva as after all it was my baptism into the male bastion. My maiden encounter with a boy as early as at the age of twelve led me to discover the physical powers. This lonely, suffering girl had a boy who left his signature on her lips and perhaps that was the moment of my life and I kept going back to it.

That night I was sleepless, cuddling into the bed and I kept going back to the moment of the kiss and whenever I opened my eyes I found Ravish right before me. I was happy; satisfied as no longer I had the pain of being left out, being an untouchable for I was touched, felt and kissed. Now the thought of Mausi irritated me as I did not want her to come and take me away. I wanted to be there, in the waiting arms of Ravish, to be kissed again, to be hugged, to be visited wherever he wanted to visit. There was complete resignation in the air, a complete submission to my airy-fairy desires and a total subjugation to the will of the man. I thought of myself being a girl and still having no remorse for whatever done by him. I wanted more and more of it, I wanted repeated kisses, and as many as possible for that was something that relieved me of a major pressure of being unwanted, of sitting on the fences of life, of being a child who had no connections to history, time and place. The break came and went. Mausi picked me up and did everything a mother does for her child during the break and brought me back to the same school after the vacation was over. Throughout the vacation, I missed Ravish and that single kiss had enthused some life into this body to be through without him for the period of vacation. Gradually Ravish crept into my soul and we almost became one life and two bodies and the school was soon agog with the news of the romance between him and me. I did not bother for I wanted to lose myself into him, to redeem myself by having some holy plunges with him. I lost my virginity that did not ail me. I loved him and I could do anything for him. I soon realized the emergence of Ravish changed the course of my life and no longer was I a weeping philosopher or a disillusioned girl. I had the satisfaction of falling into his arms, of being admired by him. Time rolled on and I passed out of the school, so did Ravish and before he left for USA, he hugged me hard, his hot tears rolled and drifted on my cheeks and he cried on the verge of separation with words, "I will come back, you must wait for me and I knew these are the words, mere words to carry me through in the daily conduct of my life." But before he left he raised me in confidence, geared me up to negotiate the dark alleys of life, inspired me to the beauty of life, unravelled the glorious mysteries of life through sex, through relationship and through those sentiments that reenergized a hapless, screaming girl. Thanks to Ravish who discovered my youth, my fancy, and my power to transform myself. Life was never so beautiful. His exit taught me to be my own self, my individuality was his gift. Now I don't care what my father did to me, what my mother denied me for everything was compensated by the love that Ravish had for me.

# Baba

Baba, clad in a snow-white Dhoti and equally starched kurta sat on the verandah with a hookah held in the left hand and the morning sun reflecting on his glossy kurta and drifting to the wall. The radiance suggested the awe and the splendour of the man who looked bright with streaks of light and the lips as though lipstick painted but it was the beetle juice tucked into the mouth and parts of it dripping down to the lower lip. That was Baba, the handsome Baba, the opulent Baba, the Baba of yester years and the Baba of his prime. Today he was there in the same fashion, waiting for all Babus of the princely state, Babus of the self created amphitheatre, of the same circle that pulled them together in a string of lost gloss and the lost extravaganza but the shards and the shades of its remnant sufficed to foster the deceptive aura of over lordship.

I had seen Baba whipping lashes on the back of Mungra and Bhudia and ripping the blouse of Chotki Rakho and the dangerously young Shyamli whom Aiyya had once discarded from the fleet of her maids for her close proximity to Baba. And then there was a literal war between the two and they almost lost each other for months together as still I could remember that the two had moved to different rooms and I was handed over to Kalawati for vigilance and protection from all troubles. Though I was small and tender, just a boy, who had opened his eyes under the weight of opulence, arrogance, aggression of the then masters and was raised like a prince. I hardly remember I ever slept between Aiyya and Baba, for I was dispatched to the care of the Au pair and Aiyya seldom bothered to see whether I was crying in the wake of night or whether mother at all was required to see the child being raised by the orderlies. But Baba was wending his way to all pleasures of life, to the celebration of all that he had garnered through his regency and through his relationship with the white Babus who doled out things in lieu of Baba's treachery with his own country and countrymen. Baba never had any remorse.

The British rule rewarded amply and suitably everyone for supporting it and going against the national movement for the liberation. Baba was a Jagirdar with acres of land accruing him for his loyalty to the British Raj. He was the main component in the scheme of compliance to the wishes of the mighty British political will to subdue the sovereignty of a nation rising to national consciousness. Baba had all scorns for the people he thought are engaged in the national movement. Gandhi he disliked thoroughly, Nehru was hated by all in his family and Sardar Patel was the most condemned name for his role in mobilizing the national opinion against the British Raj. He would often hold a newspaper in his hand and while skimming through it would abuse all those creating troubles for the Hukumat. He was furious at times and his lingoes would not spare even the national heroes. The British Raj is right for the country and see these people are smart enough to govern the nation. Look, why this Gandhi came back from South Africa, he created too many troubles there and now he is into all that nonsense here. And this Patel, what the hell does he think of himself. Bloody, he will die his own death and will lead the country to destruction. All these will be applauded by the stooges around, those living on his bread, on his charity, on his generosity, especially Ramcharan Singh, who could never afford a no to his designs, to all his absurdities and whatever was said by him was readily agreed upon. For me it was a common sight as all the discards would converge on him and shower him with the choicest words of adulation and Baba drunk with a false sense of vanity would look around with collar raised. Though I was not young enough to understand all these and the kind of celebrations that were on but somehow the mind of a child could not appreciate the arrogance of his own father and the way a host of people enjoyed his hospitality and made use of his contacts to the British Raj. I remember Hari Shankar's sister Kavita, kept coming to Baba on one pretext or the other and since she was moderately educated, Baba got her an employment in a local government school as a teacher and the price she paid for it is a common guess. I was growing with all such things at the back of my mind and whenever I looked at Aiyya I had a strange feeling that why Aiyya has been silently watching these things without any protest and whenever there was one, the crisis of relationship assumed some menacing dimensions. There were many girls employed as maids and all of them competed with each other for Baba's attention and Baba was always quick to call Saraswati who was perhaps best of the lot in terms of constitution. Deep dark eyes, a white round face, hair unkempt neatly dressed, tall legs, and a lovely body, over fed and dangerously blooded. Aiyya disliked her thoroughly and most of the times she called her a rogue for her unkempt hair. I grew fast and from school days to the college period we remained in a mansion, a huge mansion where to be lost was too easy and one of the problems Aiyya had, was to be in a huge house where it was entirely difficult to trace who is doing what and where the people have disappeared. Aiyya was on the second floor and she had the possession of three rooms, all were huge and adjacent to it was mine and there I remained with my maid or Au pair, Kalawati, who was whitish, a short stride, eyes hazel, shinning and the face had a husky look. I slept with her until I was twelve and it never occurred to me that I was sleeping with a young girl while I was myself inching towards adolescence. My sexuality at the age of twelve was totally dormant as the school I went to was boys, the outside society was not accessible to me and the only interface I had was either with Aiyya or the maids. Once I had seen Kalawati attired in a saree and her pallu just fell down and I saw her blouse with a pair of balls. That raised my curiosity and out of sheer ignorance I did ask her as why the part just above the waist appeared to be inflated to which Kalawati had smiled and promised me to tell why was it so. Kalawati was a conduit for me, a close friend, a confidante and a trustworthy pal in whom I could confide things I could have told none. Even some of the things that were so personal I had to tell it to her and she sometimes communicated it to Baba with her interpolations. Soon I moved to a college. Baba wanted me to be admitted to a college in Bhilai where the Engineering College had a good reputation but Aiyya insisted that I finish my plus two from the school and then there will be some discussions about my career to which Baba had agreed without any argument. I stayed back home and with Kalawati, the same Kalawati who was now my guide and a friend who even decided what should I take in lunch and what should I wear for the school. So things gradually fell in her hand, I too realized, that since Aiyya was more inclined to leave me in the hands of Kalawati for she was so pre-occupied with Baba and his deeds and misdeeds that she never had the time to see where was I and into what.

That was a hot noon, I just returned from the school and usually the first thing I do was to walk into the toilet either to change or other needs that I were to attend to .As I walked into the bathroom, pushing apart the ajar door, I seemed to be in for a major shock. Kalawati stood right under the shower, all bare and the tap overhead unleashed torrents of water on her body white as milk. I turned around and hurried out of the washroom. My eyes were wide open to the bizarre scene, yes bizarre for I had not seen anything like that. I could recollect the parts I had seen. A pair of milky white breasts, hands wrapped across it and the tits were still visible to me. That was perhaps the moment I was initiated into the era of sensationalism. I found that there was some sensation between the legs and some kind of heaviness was creeping into it but still I was not sure what it was. May be a physical change being induced by the descending puberty. Kalawati came out of the washroom perfectly normal and she did not look at all disturbed for whatever I had seen. I take a nap after lunch usually. That lunch I could not eat properly as my eyes kept going back to the scene of the washroom. I finished my lunch half heartedly and hurried to the room for the usual nap. Even the nap that was so dear to me giving me a slip and I was left restless in the bed with the same sensation between the legs coming back to me. Kalwati had observed the discomfiture within me. She came to the room, put the latch on and I watched her helplessly do this. After she put the latch on, she just told me that today she will make her promise good. Soon she took her kurta off, as she did it I could notice something fluffy with sharp points at the bottom making its way. My eyes were shocked and I could not believe this. She asked me to come towards her and I followed like an obedient pupil. As I went close to her, she took my hands and placed them upon her inflated stuff. This is called breast, you little, ignorant master. As I touched them, I felt, it was soft, smooth and pressed a finger on it to find whether it really goes inward. It did but soon back to the same position. My heart was furious, beating abnormally and I could clearly sense my dick going heavy, firm and rising. Kalawati was unmindful of it. She dropped my hand and put kurta on. But honestly I never wanted her Kurta to be back in place. That was the moment of my life. Kalawati after having introduced me to the novel sensation left the room and I was busy recollecting myself.

Those were the days when the freedom movement was going in full swing and the country was in the throes of a national fervour and the streets were agog with the chanting of Gandhi and Nehru, the two heroes involved in the national struggle. Quit India movement picked up rage and intensity. The British Raj was desperate and the vision of freedom seemed round the corner. Ramcharan Singh and Baba squatted on the courtyard discussing the actions of the leaders and how they were forcing the foreign rule on the back foot. I had seen the strain on Baba's face and it was more than evident that he was no longer a happy man, concerned obviously about the post independent India that did not leave any space for a man like him who would be despised and divested of all his authority and the resources. Gandhi was igniting the final spark and the whole of India was chanting the slogan, quit India movement. Ramcharan Singh found it too disconcerting to believe that the golden era of the British Raj would come to an end and thereby the golden period of their life was into the final flickers. I for one was happy since I had attained the wisdom at fifteen to understand what slavery means and how the country was being ruled by those who were not its constituent. Once I had even expressed my reservations to my Baba when there was a discussion going on between Baba and his coterie about the possibilities of self determination. I was inclined to believe having read the history books that India, my own country had been on the receiving end. First it was the Moghals who plundered and held the country hostage and now it is the Britons wreaking havoc and devastating the country. I had questioned to the best of my limited wisdom as to why Baba is so adverse to the idea of the native freedom and perhaps I thought that Baba had been enjoying all the goodies of life under the Britons and once it was curtains for them would mean Baba losing all the importance and glamour he was bestowed upon him by the Britons for acts of treachery and treason. I wondered whether I was the son of a traitor whom history will call as a treacherous fellow who ditched his own country only to enjoy the beauty and bounty of life while the rest of the sons of the soil were burning their blood to see the dawn of a new tomorrow. I felt some kind of restlessness within and thought soon Baba may realize his follies and join the same movement as the rest of the country. Baba was a die hard, who could never entertain the idea of self governance because it would have been the death of his dreams, his mighty empire would have crumbled and the luxury of life would have been replaced by the gory face of poverty. Baba, was restless those days and the British rule did not have the time to see what it could have done to ensure Baba's reverie. As the time went on the hostilities kept rising towards the Britons and the anti-Briton sentiment every nationalist harboured. I had moved to Bhiliai to join the Engineering College and as a first year student I saw the waves the freedom movement was making and the students taking to the streets with national flags fluttering in their hand and the words like "Angrezo Bharat Chodo" kept ricocheting my ears reminding me of my family associations and the background. I thought I was insulted day in and out and the burden on my conscience to be the son of a traitor played havoc with me. I was beginning to hate myself, denounce myself and wanted to redeem myself of the sins committed by my own Baba. On Sundays students of the College would congregate outside the gate and from there the procession would march towards the main city shouting slogans all the way "Angrezo Bharat Chodo". I also used to be there with my own battered conscience and with a sense that perhaps if I do my bit as a nationalist student, it may lessen the sins of my Baba. I was fear stricken for I did not want to be identified as the son of a traitor, as the son of one despised by history and condemned by conscience. I thought, freedom will be not only the freedom from the British rule but also a much savoured freedom from the likes of Baba and his caucus. The procession with young and fervent students prepared to lay their lives for the earth they belonged to was a very satisfying sight for me for I wanted to be relieved of the trauma of my own origin and history. I shouted the same slogan with all my might and strength and the more I shouted the more I felt like for I was working to redeem my Baba from the burden of a sin. Freedom seemed a realistic possibility and the British Empire kept yielding to the pressures and finally it was just a reality. It was a disconcerting reality, a reality that turned Baba's night sleepless. I kept calling him and informing him of the developments and he himself seemed well informed. Aiyya, was cool, relaxed and she thought the political freedom for the country was her own freedom from the Baba's excesses, she was more drawn towards Baba's retreat from the life of extravagance, a retreat from the life of booze and women. All these I thought would comfort Aiyya and finally she would recover her man, the same man who barely produced one son. Her nights will be hers and her husband would be hers.

I thought, and thought incessantly that night and since everyday a new trouble was brewing it appeared to me that while my involvement with the freedom movement was only symbolic and even if I were not a part of the procession it would make no difference to the agitators. I decided to see Baba and go to Laxminagar. My idea was to see the changing pattern of Baba's conduct, Aiyya's long wait to get her man back and of course Kalawati who too is a part of my life. I was thrilled at the very thought of meeting Kalawati for whatever reasons but it was certain that I found myself pushed deep into this relationship though it was not physical. I had entertained thoughts of making this relationship physical also for she had baptized me into the physical fires and now it will be she only who has to extinguish the accumulating fire within. I packed up and left for Laxminagar, for that huge mansion where nationalism was a forbidden idea, where freedom movement was a burden and where to be a nation loving man was like the unwanted guest and a burden on the family conscience. While boarding the train I thought of Baba's reaction to whatever I was going to talk about the agitations, demonstrations, protests and the very call to quit India movement and again it would be interesting to see the reactions I would be eliciting from Baba and Aiyya's silent agreement with everything I would say. It thrilled me a bit and I thought now I can discuss the aversions of Baba and the coterie he had built around himself to be regaled and to revel in false vanity. Kalawati, kept calling me. I could hear her voice, I could remember the pallu of her sari falling down, I could recall how I barged into the open washroom while she was under the shower and it really excited me. By six o' clock I would be home. I checked time and found the distance still is too much that too in the normal course and if there are disruptions by the agitators on way then it is infinite. Somehow I had to endure the pain and keep talking to the self.

By ten however I was home. From a distance I could feel the gloom visiting the wide sprawling campus and once the hub of all that Baba did today was looking so badly out of elements. The security guards that used to bark like dogs at the sight of any forward movement were sitting quiet at the gate and they were not many, just a handful. The gaggle of girls that were so visible even from outside seemed to be missing from there and there only I thought whether Kalawati too has left or chucked out. That nearly sunk my heart. But I had the conviction that Kalawati cannot do it regardless of Baba's decision and Aiyya's century old enmity with her. I stepped in rather sedately with pressed legs into the mansion and cantered into my room. It was so quiet out there that nobody took any notice of my entry into the mansion. I put my luggage on the ground and looked around to find anybody there. But quietness told itself badly. I peeped into the room of Aiyya. She was there sitting on an armchair flipping through a magazine. Next to her was Chotki Rakho squatting on the ground and gently pressing her legs. I got into the room and saluted Aiyya. Aiyya, I called and she having seen me stood up abruptly and rushed towards me to plant a kiss on my right cheek. A maiden kiss perhaps as long as I could remember or maybe she might have kissed me when I was too young. I thought since I was away from her for quite sometime, the mother within her was stirred a bit. I asked her, about Baba and his health. I thought Aiyya would be too delighted to tell or guide me to his direction. But she wore a smile and whispered, he is in his room. Infact all these appeared to me to be buying time for the one I was looking for. I thought she would call Kalawati and direct her to do things for me. But I was surprised to see her walking into the kitchen herself with Chotki Rakho. Again my heart went for a toss and I was getting desperate. There was no trace of Kalawati around and a host of apprehensions ran across my mind and I was figuring out whether at all Kalawati has been chucked out in the wake of Baba's declining influence. I gave a jerk to my mind and consoled myself that Kalawati cannot leave without telling it to me. My confidence perhaps had no basis because it was not a love relationship and whatever I thought, I thought on the basis of an emotional crisis that had crept early into my life for the parental indifference. I went back to my room and threw myself on the bed closing eyes. There was an uneasy calm that hung around the room. I watched everything carefully. Things were exactly the way I had left them. That means, I held on, Kalawati perhaps, perhaps ...

Chotki Rakho just got into my room with a tray studded with loads of edibles. I asked her to put them on the table and leave. But before that just a thought occurred to me that she is the best person to tell me about Kalawati. I ordered her gently to sit down and she sat there on the ground. It did seem to me that there was something she wanted to tell as she kept looking at the entrance point of the room. I interrupted and ran out of patience. Chotki, I addressed her with all politeness. Maaji. Maaji, I was surprised. What Maaji. She is here. What for, somehow I could muster. I saw Aiyya, coming towards me. Hi, boy, what are you upto and why things are lying there. Look, I have prepared this breakfast for you. Please wash yourself and finish it off fast. You must have lost the taste of everything for that Kalawati never knew cooking and fed you the things you would have thrown but I really feel sorry for that, my son. My heart took another nosedive and now I was more than convinced that Kalawati has left but how could she do it to me. She was my best friend under this sun, the one who shared my secrets, the one saw me walking into the corridors of youth, the one who knew all about me. How she could do this to me? It sounded incredible. I promised Aiyya to finish my breakfast and I asked her to leave Chotki there so that she takes things back and bring coffee for me. Aiyya left having augmented my concerns. I stood up and edged up towards Chotki, very close to her ear, where is Kalawati. I whispered. Chotki, smiled, and I had to smile back; I again pressed the same question into her ear. What happened to her? Where is she? All these questions were fired in the urgency of soliciting a reply from her but that witch, Chotki was delaying purposefully what I wanted to know from her. She is here. What. I jumped with the flair of happiness, that happiness that told itself on my face and I could sense the cunning smile of Chotki. Babu, I will go and tell her that you are here. I shot another question. Doesn't she know that I am here? Perhaps not. Maaji does not allow her to move into Bada Saab's room and she just stays downstairs. Why, I asked with an open mouth. Ok, Saab, I will go and tell Kalawati about you. Yeah, yeah. She left and left me thinking. I finished my breakfast, took coffee and still there was no news about Kalawati. I was getting nervous though I was yet to see Baba. I again went into the room of Aiyya and told her that I am going to see Baba and much to my surprise she expressed a desire to join me. She took my hand, hers was warm, very warm, and almost escorted me into Baba's room. Baba was lying on the bed, pale, sapped of blood, the wrinkles were visible, the beetle juice tucked under his mouth, spectacle on, and a plethora of newspapers waited for scansion. I saluted him and he blessed me with his eyes. What I discovered there, were, the two beds attached to each other and I could identify the things that belonged to Aiyya comfortably resting on the bed, her spectacle, the book of Geeta, her Hindi magazines etc etc. I looked towards Aiyya and she almost nodded as if she got what I was gazing at. I was there for a while with Baba and I wanted to ask Baba or tell him something about the freedom movement but Baba was more focused on the newspapers and I took his leave and came back to my room. Still nothing was heard from Kalawati and I hurled choicest abuse on Chotki for her let down. I thought she, did not tell anything to Aiyya. I was not supposed to go into a maid's room and talk to her there since it was against the ethics of the family. I was helpless and kept looking at the door, waiting for the sounds of the much wanted footsteps. I almost slept.

A gentle, muffled and delicate tinkling of the bangles visited my dormant consciousness and I stretched out my hands to find access to the onrushing sounds and felt a very warm, tender, voluptuous, amply blooded hand brushing my forehead. My eyes were closed, I could feel the sensation, I could sense the effable touch, the elegance of cunningly crafted fingers running all over my face, the typical but familiar body odour of a young girl with whom I slept until my adolescence. I did not want to open my eyes but enjoy the fabulous feminine caress. The running fingers widened their canvass as they rolled down to my cheeks, to my neck, to my eyes and I was in a trance. Still the eyes refused to open for I did not want to spoil the beauty of the moment. My God, what fingers were they. Thin as paper, weightless, pointed with a rare finesse and appeared to be finely crafted with total precision and power. Very soon I could feel the warm breath colliding with my lips, burning lips had all fire in it. Restless, and transported, I gradually unfolded my eyelashes, still trying to preserve the sanctity, the beauty and the rarity of the moment. I felt the same heaviness creeping between my legs, the hard stuff rising and struggling for space. Kalawati, bended and left a kiss on a pair of lips. I enjoyed that kiss, the kiss of the life, the kiss of all joy and the kiss of bliss for a depraved and emotionally shattered body. I flicked my hands around her face. Then to her lips, put a finger in her mouth, the saliva drooled out and the same finger I crashed against my lips. It had a taste difficult to explain its nature. Kalawati, driven by the fire of youth almost melted into me and I went back to the scene of the washroom where I had seen her bathing with nothing on. It was a rehash, a re-enactment of the same scene but the difference was in me for now I was a youngman with all the energies of youth. I visited her crammed space, examined the fluffy and flowing stuff with a lot of flesh on it and got the feel of the quivering points. They were dark as night and while the rest of the flesh reminded me about the falling morning dew in a winter morning.

That encounter with youth awakened me to the reality of the celebration of life and that was not the only one. Noon's were devoted religiously to those encounters and there I discovered the beauty of life and attained my salvation. Kalawati never looked so beautiful again.

It was 1947 and India was freed from the yoke of slavery and with the declaration of independence, Baba lost his freedom to be free of his entire rule, authority and the wedding to luxury came to an abrupt end. All his coterie disappeared in a single day and the luxuries of yesterday went on to become the worries of today. Divested of his wealth, condemned as a traitor and ridiculed as a British stooge, Baba almost renounced life and death gained upon him furiously. Aiyya was finally relieved of the bondage of human pain and her feminism asserted itself in the wake of Babas fall from the grace. I too had the satisfaction that no longer I will have to endure the pain of being one with a burden on his conscience. Kalawati disappeared in the storm of independence as all maids one after another were chucked out under the duress of onrushing poverty.

# Rupture

Slowly her steps picked up pace, she wanted to move forward but somehow the thought of the one held her back as if she was negotiating the muddy and slushy roads fraught with the impending danger of doom. She was likely to be doomed for the one basically short on decision making ability suffers for centuries and she was bound to suffer. The suffrage, the element of self doubt and the intense desire to scale the walls of shackles imposed by the mores of the day, dividing the human beings into conflicting identities, communities and the adherence to age old creed, rotten, as the time, itself occupied the mind space of Prerna, so much that she almost took a wrong step. She was not the kind who would twitter and chirp the way a bird in frenzy sings in her own language. Spoke very little or say neither need based, while alone never spoke to the self, nor ever a harsh word even for those who tormented her. A demure looking with fancy staggering to release itself from the bounds of quitude, she never knew she was an individual with some flesh and blood in it. The air of resignation to the things around summed up her approach to the life she lived under the duress of her own being.

From the childhood days, Prerna, was a very different child. She did not find the thrill of life, somewhat brooding possibly on the things around or watching the world from the distance as if the circumstances of her life had something in them to make her so withdrawn. She had a sparkling pair of eyes and she probed the conditions of her existence with them. Early on while going to the school she was impressed by a sister and somehow felt close to her. Her class was enthralling for her, her words left some deep impact on her mind and she fell in some kind of a unification with her. There was nobody around who could fathom the depths of her loneliness or the agony of being for a sensitive child it is never easy to come to terms with the seemingly indifferent aura. She was thinking but a resigned child, the aggression within her perhaps did not exist. Being too recessive and too circumspect Prerna took everything in her stride. From the school days religion never impressed her. She did not find the urgency to run to a temple and seek whatever was within her. An Aryasamaji to the core with conservatism descending upon her as a matter of inheritance, her parents were the devotees of Lord Hanumaan. A strictly vegetarian family cannot find much food for thought as the blood goes green and the body is decisively short on certain vitamins. Her brothers Joy and Harish took no notice of the sister seemingly upset with a life yet to find the gales of giggles. Joy was particularly severe on her with his mocking abilities. Calling her dull, neurotic and devoid of common wisdom ailed and pained Prerna but she never protested. Her father PKS never had the time from his profession to attempt a peep into the sedate life of his daughter. There are fathers in the oriental set up who leave the management of a daughter's life to the hands of mothers. His wife Sangeeta was moderately educated; out and out a homely woman whose priorities were the two sons and the daughter came as an afterthought. Confining the movements of the daughter from college to home and still keeping vigilance from the closed walls of the house she never thought her daughter Prerna, has a heart that bleeds, has a mind that thinks and has wisdom that makes her question things around. Keeping away from the boys, not inclined to send her away from the town for the higher education for it was the domain of the sons who could have career of their choices. Prerna, watched all in a relative state of indifference and never lodged her protest. A chanced child perhaps not taken very kindly within its own fold had to find reasons to talk to her father. The gap between the daughter and the father was more than traditional.

That was a long, dark night and the rain came down at an intimidating pace. Prerna, confined to the sounds of the falling rain stretched out her hands from the window rods to get the feel of the raindrops only to be intercepted by the shout of her mother. Prerna, close the window and come to me. Even though the small raindrops that she was collecting on her palm had formed a bubble had to be shunned there only since she was ordered to close the window by her mother. This Prerna, did not like for she was even not allowed to watch the falling rains. She thought her life is as torrential as the falling rains. She went quiet again and the smile that seemed to appear on her lips on the scene of the falling rain lost its ways as if somebody has given a knock at the wrong door. Sangeeta, was adventurous in terms of going out, meeting people, defying vegetarianism to infuse some life into her drying saliva by sneaking into her parental house every now and then and going for the forbidden fruit. Her parents lived in the same town and that was something she liked best about her own self. By nature she was talkative, modest, and unlike her daughter she did not bury things in her heart. She acted smarter than she was though without the exposure to any meaningful institution. Her daughter was antithesis to her; she was a model of compliance and hardly ever thought her happiness is also a thing to be desired. Sangeeta had only one problem to contend with, the octogenarian father in law. The man was old and particularly severe on his schedule and maintaining the schedule of the old man was quite a problem for her. Oldies have a typical knack of hanging on to the life even though there is hardly any sense being a burden on those around. The westerners are very smart to dump them in the old house and be free of the daily hassles but the oriental women are so bound by the values that whether they like it or not they have any choice but to see to it that the old man does not suffer. The cringing was always there and she was furious at times and the words like, this old man will live on to send us back, is older than Taj Mahal though the colour of the Taj Mahal has faded but this man is strong enough to survive all season. Prerna would listen to all these and leave a word or two like if you don't want to do, then why don't you tell to papa that service is not possible and you cannot do it to which Sangeeta would react, shut up, all you have to do is to comment. What you do? Just pick up your bag and leave for college. Prerna would just be mum for she knew further arguments were of no use.

There was one more problem in Prerna's house, the continuous flow of guests. Since the elder brother of her father was a very reserved person and his sisters in town did not bother much for those coming from their native village, Prerna's house was literally turned into "Dharamshaala. That further tortured Sangeeta, and she would blurt at the spectacle of a guest and find it almost unmanageable though she had the ready assistance of Prerna. All those who had nowhere to go from Balrampur went on to become the official guest of PKS in Patliputra. Sangeeta, was sick of playing host, and cursed at times her fate for being the member of such a family. Amid all these the life of Prerna, kept going without the required sense of direction. Her admission to the local College of Arts was the natural choice her parents had and Prerna too did not make any bone out of it. The college year began. The year one of the three years degree course had no excitement for Prerna and there was hardly any hue and cry for attendance. Prerna in the year one did not experience the fancy of a young college going student and when the year came to an end, she hardly realized that. It was only in the second year of the degree course that Prerna developed some friendship and the girls like Anjali, Konica, Shivani, became her regular friends and the three of them specially rummaged through the campus together. There the life of Prerna seemed to be in for a change and the winds of change blew so fast that it even rattled her up. College of Arts had some very good and qualified teachers in its fold and particularly the English department had the rare distinction of seven women at the helm. They were good teachers with some brilliant looks too. Clad in stiffly starched Cotton Sari, heavily painted and perfumed bodies, the eye lashes decently decorated and the personality stood in impeccable shape. It was not that there were only female teachers. It was huge department of fifteen members and the balance tilted slightly in favour of the men. Eight plus seven that is to suggest the slender lead of the male teachers. Also the general atmosphere of the College of Arts and Science was better in comparison to the other colleges of the city. Male and female teachers specially the young ones met freely, moved on the campus without reservations and electrified the atmosphere with their distinct humour. On the first sight it might appear to the visitor that all relations are beyond the common standards of acceptance and might go back with the impression that the male teachers of the College are flirts. But it was wrong in the sense that beyond the free movement there was nothing to look at otherwise that would have rendered the lives of the husbands sleepless.

Prerna seemed to be enjoying her days at college in the year two of the same degree course. She was short, innocence dripped from her face, the eyes oozed radiance, soft spoken and she exuded confidence required to conduct her. She took some measured steps forward, in the realm of future that held all terrors. The lectures at the College of Arts and Science were quite regular and the teachers by and large knew their responsibilities. Among many there was one fellow called Saam. Short in height, round faced arrogant looking individual had all the talent in the world to impress upon the princess of beauty and wit. Himself witty, his one liner was an instant hit, was mostly seen in the company of women teachers who never took his jibes, quirks and quips seriously. In a way he had the license to intrude into any department and hold the hand of the lady teachers partly to tease the senior generation teachers and partly to leave an impression to his colleagues that they should not dare the same or else the flying sandals will be the scene of the day. None infact dared but envied him from the depth of their hearts. Saam was known to be a well meaning individual and if anybody ran after him it were the students. They took particular note of his lectures, they remembered the days and time of his classes. One of the things that he himself was particular, the eagerness to be with the students, their problems and shared their burden. KPS was the chairman of the department and he considered him ready cash. But Saam was inconsistent in the sense that he always wanted to jump on the global academic scene by accepting overseas assignments. Going to the far end of the world was high on his agenda and he seemed more than willing to execute it. The students despised the idea and whenever he discussed the issue in the classroom there were some dazed faces as if they are not ready to be through the crisis. It happened twice. On much insistence of the students Saam had given his email id to them. The serious ones thought that to be the "golden key of a golden gate" that were to unearth later on a long tale mired in unimaginable pain. That was also the beginning of an era of optimism, exuberance, understanding the human values and how human relations can transcend the barriers of time, space and religion.

Prerna looked too out of sorts from the moment Saam made it known to the students that shortly he will be leaving for the overseas assignment. Prerna in particular seemed not the usual self though, from her expressions it was more than clear that she did not like the idea at all. But Saam unmindful of who thinks what went ahead with his programmes. Days went fast as if they were like an express train on a specially designed track.

The October vacation was round the corner and Saam was to leave during the vacation only and his last working day happened to be just a day before the vacation since he was already granted the leave-cum lien for a period of one year liable to further extension. All seemed quiet and settled but there was somebody thoroughly unsettled, not inclined to believe the existing reality but Saam knew nothing about it except the fact that he was loved by his students and his exit was a certain loss to them strictly in terms of academics. There was something personal about something, he could not understand and this perhaps had some reflections on the last day of his college. As he walked into the classroom on the final day, he was greeted with a very emotional good morning and he could have observed the strain on some faces and the most on a particular face. He thought these girls are very career oriented and perhaps he could have helped them reach out to their destinations. As he wanted to polish off the remains of his syllabus, he encountered the drops of tear dripping on a face and she was struggling to check the tears on the rampage. Saam many a time in the classroom had observed the movement of Prerna's' eyes, the eye contact, the flickering flame of emotions overpowering them and the acute presence of a girl who never took her eyes off him. Since he was a professor not looking beyond what really meets the eyes but somehow he admonished the thoughts as the fabrication of his over productive imagination. Prerna's eyes were not free of some drops of acid accruing from swollen eyes. Saam was convinced that this girl has taken things to her heart and there was a profound touch of grief. Those tears had the message of the human association, the warmth of tender emotions, the elegance of innocuous heart and deep down the pains of a supposed separation. Somehow she was dispatched home but before that she bled profusely literally. That was perhaps the beginning of a tale replete with hundred possibilities. Saam too felt the burden on his heart and the tears gushing out form her eyes at regular intervals impelled him to think the most irrelevant thing. But was that an irrelevant exercise, or was that the beginning of a turbulent tale? Saam had the sense of heaviness and his heart time and again ran out to the same sobbing girl who seemed to be a goddess of all innocence with a heart that pumped for the wrong man.

After some days Saam received an email from her and the telephonic conversations went on to become the order of the day. The talks mostly hovered around academics, his exit, the circumstantial collision with a girl whose emotions were going berserk and she had resigned to her fate. Infact youth is such a blind thing that it refuses to accommodate the negative possibilities. Saam scanned the email of Prerna and read it with all indifference. The mail never said the unsaid; the emotions were a bundle of youthful exuberance and the imagination seemed to create an authentic space for fancy. The mail was an acknowledgement of Saam's contributions and commitments to the cause of the students and an exaggerated version of a young mind conducting itself on a dicey platform. He was happy to be acknowledged and concerned about the aftermath of his exit on Prerna. That was perhaps the first moment for him to have entertained a thought other than academics. The confirmation of the same came later. Saam boarded the Rajdhani express and hardly had he settled down, the message beep made him check his cell. "All the best for your journey, Sir. Miss you badly" Saam read the message and thanked her though no reply was attempted for he was on the anvil of a journey that he thought, will take him beyond the rivers of emotion, beyond the fragility of feminine calls and beyond the geographical boundaries as if he was sailing on a ship with holes in it. Saam was a bit morose in the sense that though that was his own decision to leave the country but the way his elder daughter collapsed on the platform made him think whether his decision is the right one. The man who was joining him up to Delhi was his friend Jannu Bhai. He felt the discomfiture within Saam and he had his words for the occasion. Somehow the train whistled away for the destination one. As the train moved a terrain of thoughts ranging from Juhi to Prerna descended on Saam. He closed his eyes and left everything to time. The next day he had his flight from Indira Gandhi International Airport for Jeddah. The time of flight was midnight. Saam was to join as a professor of English at King Saud University, Saudi Arabia. Calls were intermittent. Wife, father mother and friends including Prerna, all bombarded Saam with calls. Just a word he would leave to all calls. Inshallah, will get back to you from Jeddah. That was perhaps 9 O' clock and Saam was speeding down the airport road since it is customary to report three hours before the schedule for visa checks, confirmation of ticket, uploading of baggage etc. Saam had been to other countries before and he knew what the international journey really meant.

Since the flight was not direct to Jeddah, Saam was to go via Bahrain. At Bahrain there was a stopover of about an hour. The connecting flight was to be boarded from there only. The flight for Jeddah was delayed by three hours which meant the connecting flight from Bahrain was never a possibility. Saam, realized the ordeal began there only. What he suspected had already happened. After four hours of the flight in the Gulf Air, he was literally broken, jetlag leaving its own scar on a crumbling body. Saam at the Bahrain airport stretched his mind back to all those affected by his adventure to the outside world. Juhi, his daughters and deep down somewhere in some form Prerna also figured. The announcement was made very soon that those who missed the flight to Jeddah can leave tomorrow only as there is no flight for the day. Shivers ran down his spine and left him seething with anger but the consolable part was the hospitality extended by the Gulf Air. Jaded to bones, Saam rushed to the hotel and was keen a bit to negotiate the roads of Bahrain. Lovely spectacle, women of all hues and colour, some of them were there at the airport. Clad as scantily as possible, lips painted solidly, as if they are done with Berger paints that no tongue can wipe, legs exposed right up to the thighs and above the waist all was left to the care of the people. Saam felt some new life being injected into the body all in shreds.

The next day the new vigour was on though all lines of communications were broken down as if he was up in the poles. After an hour he landed at the Jeddah airport. One more day, he had to be there because from there his destination was still a flight away. He along with his two colleagues who happened to meet him at the Bahrain airport bound for the same destination gave some encouragement to him. All moved together from there falling on each other's broken shoulders, the shoulders that were drooping. Saam thought that to be the right opportunity to make some connections to the disconnected ones. Made calls to Juhi, his father and Prerna were shot a mail. Just a mail to suggest he was on his way. That was enough for the growing relationship. It was also done to alley her fears regarding him since she appeared too concerned. There also I left a word that for the next one week, there would be nothing from him as he can get back to her only after he settled down. He thought, she is sensible and will get the point.

The life at Saudi took its own time to settle down as the early days are always difficult and to find the ways to a comfortable life depends on the sense of involvement with the given milieu. Saam was always a slow starter and his doubts never spared him though he was determined enough not to look back. The doubt had its own reason to exist for the kind of background his mental milieu was obsessed with did not let him think beyond the issue of settling down to the place. There had been no communication with anyone in the first few weeks of his arrival but everyone back home prayed hard that Saam does not find the place as tormenting as Libya. God eventually prevails when the going gets tough and he got along well and kept going with a mind to be firmly in the situation he was put into. The days passed without raising alarms, the life continued without the suspected jerks and Saam found the going to his taste. Sometimes life has a smooth pattern and it does not test the endurance to the hilt. So thought Saam, and gave a good response to the conditions. The thought of Prerna, was a revelation, an idea that called for some deliberations. He did not think as much about Juhi as that of Prerna who had crept into his imagination and from a formless entity to the guiding and driving impulses. The emergence of a girl over the murky horizons of a skeptical individual transformed the whole point of view about life, its turns and twists. A more confident and happy looking Saam left his skepticism behind and clung to the lovely melodies the very voice of the nightingale produced. He found himself recovering from the bouts of investigative depression and looked at the heavens only to thank it for providing the impetus to hang on to the life.

Late night talks, going back to Prerna even at the drop of a hat, reporting of whatever happened reduced Juhi to a footnote only for which Saam has had no regrets. The willing submission of Prerna to the desires of Saam introduced a new song in his life. Prerna's words like "life is unthinkable without you", "Cannot do without you", I would accept no other man in my life and the likes of it left nothing for Saam to doubt whether she could be a reality. But life is no fiction, it is no island, it is not a famished road nor is it a walk under the golden lights heaped by the golden lamps. Back home, Juhi was beginning to find some concerns for the first ever time in her life about something that ideally she would have hated to see. The development of a tale, a tale of relationship between two individuals promising to culminate in one of the finest ever told stories had to be abandoned to the fate, to the time and to the uncertain tomorrow. Prerna, a splendid creature of Nature infested with admirable gifts discovered the songs of life but sung it hesitantly for she knew she never had the strength to make it a reality. The disconnects do not ask for time, the breakdown does not come about with a careful thought and to find things slipping away from the grip happens on its own. Prema, realized soon that she would be handed over to "some" someday but never thought that it would come so abruptly. Saam was ready to force his way through, to fight with the world, to renounce life, to embrace ostracism, to walk on the dangerous roads of death but all these dwindled to a well conceived plot of a "Romantic Fiction".

The exit of Prerna from Saam's life, switched all blood from his life, took the juice out of the lemon, left him stranded on the uncertain roads, wedded him to the perennial drudgery and effectively imposed a practical ban on the smiles of life. Prerna caved in to the local pressures without making a fight of it and fastened the streets of creativity for Saam for he wrote only for his nightingale. Saam though has not lost hopes of recovering his nightingale from the adversities of time, from the passages of history, from the unseen spectacle of time and from the unholy hold of the one presiding over her destiny. But he does know that history records facts only and the one hard fact is the departure of Prerna from his life. The same life today is a burden on his conscience, is an extension of the punishment meted out by the indifferent forces but what he rues basically is the abject resignation of Prerna to the indifferent world. Had she shown a bit of spine, Saam indeed would have been singing the joyous songs of life, those songs that came close to him but still remained so far away? Today Saam lives in past, lives a wretched existence, has all the resources in the world to be happy but there is nothing for him in the absence of Prerna and therefore he writes,

"Creativity needs inspiration. And the inspiration can either be a person, or a source in a certain form that connects to the route of imagination. Creativity creeps in not in an exalted state of mind, rather a grief stricken and tension ridden thinking mind that scales the impediments of thought mechanism and conducts itself being independent of the abstract affiliations. The assumption of ideas emanates from a mind that has been tormented by the mass of experience. To sit and write is convenient and in fact very convenient. But will it have the lyrical gush or the immediacy of the language is a moot point?

Saam for one finds the route for inspiration rooted into the tender, sensational, and lyrical giggles of obscure character whose name remains mired in the solid anchoring of a human heart that staggers to pump without being aware of her presence in absentia. He was led to the corridors of creativity without ever realizing that he can really create.

Whatever sense it had, turned into nonsense exaggerated assertions of overwhelming emotions. His life has been a drama but still a great melodrama, has been a tragedy but still a great sentimental tragedy. He does not look back in anger without being appreciative of the unpalatable circumstances culminating into a disaster at a personal level. No longer the inspiration can act as a redeeming force or can suffice to salvage the declining influence that stayed at the back of the mind for a brief spell. It disappears only to reappear to remind that one's creativity was a gift accruing from a willing heart.

# The Old Man and Ganga

Ganga's steps ran on the paddy with a sense of urgency. She was almost into her strides forward without looking back the steps behind that seemed to follow her. Early morning she had a scuffle with her husband, Atma Ram, an addict to everything that produced intoxication. Atma Ram was about fifty-two, elder to Ganga who seemed not more than twenty-five or six at the most. The gloss on her face suggested she was young though ill fed, a bit of blood was still there in her body to keep her going. Atma Ram on the other hand was seduced not by the youthful body of Ganga but the streams of liquor, which ran into his belly and made it look like a bottle half filled with gurgling water. Ganga's hasty steps went on uninterrupted and moved with alacrity. At the back of her mind, the ghost of Atma Ram was playing some wild games and she lifted her lanky legs with more energy for she thought the same unworthy husband might be behind her to dissuade what she had in her mind to do

Her steps were so used to the route that even blindfolded she could negotiate it. She was a village girl, and the village Behrampur, she knew like the lines on her palm. She opened her eyes to the sun in her courtyard, she toddled on the same courtyard, learnt walking there only and held the fingers of all those who were there watching her grow up. The house was built of mud raised through the support of the bamboo streaks. Straws were piled on and spread on the terrace to stop the blazing sun and ward off the intimidating rains. Small chunks of land accrued to her father as his share in the ancestral property and that sufficed for them all. She had three sisters and two brothers with almost bare minimum gaps between them. Ganga was the eldest and the most beautiful also. Her father, Sitaram Singh died a premature death and from there the saga of unpalatable songs became an inseparable part of their life. Her brothers, Manthan and Sanathan were the two docile creatures, a burden on this earth for they sold everything to invite the ire of poverty. Both moved away to the adjoining city and since then there has been no news about them. The grapevine has it that both of them lost their lives while kidnapping a businessperson. Shekawat Rajput, an elderly man wielding some influence on the villagers and one also who had a shady role in the death of Ganga's father, churned out this tale repeatedly. He was a much-disliked man and generally despised by those whose land he had usurped. His sons Billa Shekawat, Ranjit Lotia, Mahadev Ganju were the Romeos plucking girls from all courtyards. The girls screamed when they saw them, they were molested by them and at times deflowered.

Ganga kept going with all possible haste, ran, jumped and hopped in the urgency to leave the village far behind, to leave her husband struggling for everything and to find a way that might provide her the breathing space from the tormenting milieu of her life. The shadows were creeping, the sun almost was dipping and dissolving its heat and long almost deserted stretches of land kept company. She looked around, her throat was parched, and her stomach made empty sounds, her eyes, flickered like a burning candle. She went on, lost in the streams of thought, summoning the past to comfort her bruised soul, to create a moment of succour from the burning pyre her life had turned into. She thought of her brothers supposedly dead if Shekawat's tale was to be trusted. She thought of everything but Atma Ram. She hated him to the core, disliked every bit of him. Such a repulsive face he had. She hardly remembers whether she ever had sex with him for he was a lamp that burnt its oil long back. Nevertheless, he would pull her dress down every night, stare at her bare boobs, fondle the nipples, slid his finger into the burning oven. He did everything but to nullify the heat. She thought, she would never forgive that bitch of a woman, Malti Roopali responsible for her marriage to Atma Ram. She knew everything about him but still she coerced her into this marriage. She looked at the sky. The evening was about to disappear. The sun had been lost behind while she kept moving where she was going, she did not know, as the darkness began to take control. The night did not seem too far. The half moon hung perilously as if it would fall down to the ground but she was not scared. She knew there would be some destination, some points where God will guide her to the correct route. Tired to the bones, she resigned to the ground; it was wet by the falling dew. She rolled her hands about the dew on the meadow and felt some life was creeping back into her body. She plucked a shaft of grass, put it in between her teeth and chewed it. While chewing, she felt some kind of energy for further movement. The road ahead was tough, not known either and it was getting dark. Her tongue was dried up, lips cracked under the duress of dryness and the face dipped in sweat. She stood up, held the pallu of her saree in her right hand and put herself back on the trail.

Amid darkness, the howling of the dogs rendered the scene appalling but she was on the move. After some steps were taken she saw a streak of light at a certain distance, her eyes lit up on the sight of a light, she thought may be there is a village not like Behrampur which ripped and broke her, which swept away the waves of youth and the urge to live on. Engaged in self-talks she came very close to the light. No, it was not a village, rather the block, Qasimjaan. Yes the same Qasimjaan block where her father would often come for fodder for the livestock and some seeds. She knew it though she never came here. Right before the same light Ganga took a halt; her legs shuddered almost for she had covered the distance of her lifetime. She stood before a tea stall, reset her saree and put its pallu on her head. She asked for water. There were two men sitting inside the stall that was perilously close to a free flowing clan. Both looked at her, a typical male gaze and Ganga again set her saree back in order and held the pallu on her head with her left hand. Water was served in a small tea glass. She drank that in a single go. Asked for more, infact drank five glasses on the trot. The old man who served water to her, looked at her with some compassion in his eyes. Bitiya, you seem very thirsty. Where you are coming from, the question had a tinge of sympathy. Behrampur. The old man was awe struck. You marched down to Qasimjaan from Behrampur on foot. The old man seemed too awe struck. Ganga, asked for some food. Some hot kachauris and vegetables she ate to her full satisfaction. Again drank three glasses of water as if she was gearing up for another spell of march. She untied her pallu, and put a currency of fifty rupee on the outstretched palm of the old man. He saw it, groped his fingers inside the box of money, counted it and returned it to her. Bitiya it is forty-five. Ganga took the money from the old man and came out of the stall. After water and a bit of food she brought herself back to life and was now quite prepared to face what next is in store for her. There was an immediate problem tormenting her. The problem of the night as to where she would spend it. She was confused, short of ideas that left her thinking. For a woman to be out on the road all alone in a block like Qasimjaan was asking for troubles only. However, she had no idea. She thought perhaps somebody could know her father, Sitaram Singh, who used to visit Qasimjaan frequently. But whom to ask at that odd hour of night. It was dangerous also because anybody could take her anywhere. But what to do, thought Ganga and she has to find a way out. She turned around and went back to the stall. The same old man was still there. She went close to him and with words in mouth struggled to say what she wanted to. The old man felt that there was some trouble with her. He asked her not to fear anything as he was like her father. He asked her to sit-down and relax for a while. There was a moment of silence between the two. The silence hung there as a method of communication. Two more men dropped in. Baba, please give us some tea. Both men seemed well built and the youth was present in its belligerent form. They were not very tall, somewhat short and the eyes produced a brightness that Ganga could see. They were talking and still stealing a look of the woman there. They also looked towards the old man rather suspiciously. The old man now came very close to her, almost edging up to her ear. Yes, Bitiya, what was that you wanted to say? Ganga still a bit hesitant, summoned her commonsense and asked the old man straightaway. Baba, do you know Sitaram Singh of Behrampur. The old man staggered for a while, held himself together and looked towards Ganga. Yes. Bitiya, Yes. Bitiya. Sitaram Singh was my very close friend and he always came to Qasimjaan for his needs. He used to have his breakfast at this stall only. How do you know him Bitiya, the curiosity of the old man pacified some anxious moments Ganga and now was more assured of herself. Baba, He was my father. The old man now had some more sympathy for that woman. But Bitiya you said you came from Behrampur on foot What was the urgency or the need whatever for you to do it. Baba, Ganga's voice went wet, it is a long tale, I will tell you sometime later. Ganga quickly added, Baba, I do not know where I will go tonight, as there is no safe place here. The old man interrupted, Bitiya, you are like my daughter; do not say anything like that. The old man was full of affection for Ganga. As the silence fell again between the two, the old man and Ganga, the two youths almost ran into Ganga.They held themselves together somehow, leaned towards her and one of the youths put his hand on Ganga's head with utmost affection that left Ganga bewildered. The old man was also somewhat flummoxed about the situation. Are you the daughter of Sitaram Singh of Behrampur? Ganga was further dazed and before she could do anything, the two men looked into the eyes of the old man. Hey, Baba, look at this strange coincidence. The woman who is seeking protection from you is infact my sister, Ganga, my own sister. Ganga seemed to lose her blood again for this was something that only bewildered her further. The old man was not very excited for he suspected some foul play. The two youths were asked to sit down and then the old man turned towards Ganga, took her hand and went out of the stall. There was an old woman outside the stall. He handed over Ganga to her and asked her to take her home. Soon Ganga realized the old woman was his wife. She too was very affectionate. As the old woman reached her home made of stacks of bricks and steel, there were two young girls outside and they received Ganga with all affection.

The old man came after sometime with the two men who were claiming Ganga to be their sister. Ganga was tired, fatigued as every inch of her body cried out of pain, sheer pain. The two men turned out to be the sons of Sitaram Singh as they gave enough evidence to the old man to dispel his doubts. Ganga broke down completely. Cried at the top of her voice, Baba, Baba, see your, sons are alive, they are alive. She hugged them hard as if she would not spare them from her clutches. The two men were wiping tears from their eyes and the old man, consigned to a corner was seen muttering, Sitaram Singh, don't worry, your daughter and sons are in my safe hands.

# Jassu, the Winner

Rashmi ran all day long to procure the form of B.Ed as she was advised to do this course by her ailing father. She never wanted to do it for she was committing herself to pursue medicine but the deteriorating health of her father interfered with her soaring ambitions. She brought herself down to the brute reality of the demands of poverty from the garden of fantasy. Her father Nisith Narayan was a primary school teacher in the small village of Dumrisarai. However, he was not very old but the wounds inflicted by the paucity of financial resources reduced him to a skeleton of a man. He took staggering steps holding the umbrella in one hand and a tattered bag with umpteen holes in the other. It was customary for him to carry the two things, one as a shield against the sun and rain while the other was to put some vegetables at the end of the day. His wife, Rukmani was a devoted homemaker raising and rearing five children. All daughters. Sometimes the two would sit together for hours engaged in intimate discussions about the probable future of the kids and they would sound rather pathetic since they felt the resources available are much less than required. Five daughters can only be a disaster but Nisith Narayan kept his moods upbeat, looked towards the heaven and uttered few words of faith in his agency. He will do it all. Rukmani, you know, Jaidev Babu had seven daughters and he never had any problem. He gave only moderate education to them and all of them were wedded to decent boys and families. He raised his hands and again expressed his faith in his God. Narayan does things his own way. Rukmani's silence was a manifestation of the faith in her husband's unflinching submission to God. Nisith Babu, Nisith Babu. The call was repeated by Shambunath, the peon of school. Rashmi, Rashmi, Nisith Narayan shouted from his room and Rashmi came running. Yes. Babuji. Bitiya, see, Shambunath is there at the door. Please call him in, offer him some water and tea. I would be there shortly. Rashmi ran to the door and humbly requested him to come inside. Shambunath was holding a folded paper in his hand. In addition, having seen her, he handed over the paper to her. I went to the block today to get this form for you. Nisith Babu had told me to bring it for you. I have also taken one for my Bitiya., Bindu. Rukmani stood her ground for a while, thought a thing or two and disappeared from there. There was something going in her mind but this was very disturbing also. Shambunath is a Dalit and his daughter Bindu studying or doing the same course with her, oh my God, what is this. She thought to question her father but dropped the idea to be silently through the ordeal. Nisith Narayan was a Brahmin by caste, the upper Hindu hierarchy though poverty hardly ever allowed him to see himself as the one much revered in terms of the social status. Nevertheless, his daughters did nurse at the back of their subconscious a feeling that they are the chosen ones albeit seldom celebrated it. The thought of mingling with a Dalit girl ailed Rashmi a bit and deep down she completely disliked the very scene of being with her. Shambunath though does drink and eat at her home but his mother keeps separate utensils for him without the knowledge of Nisith Narayan.

It was a soggy evening as short spells of rain rendered everything sluggish. Nisith Narayan an orthodox Hindu had diluted much of his Puritanism under the changing conditions. Gone were the days when a Dalit would resign to the outskirts of the village, bow before every ordinary man of the upper caste and salute all and sundry. The government introduced a host of measures to emancipate them socially and the ostracism ceased to be a reality. This ailed all much the same way but the changing polity had the final say. Only recently, the government announced that any exploitation of the Shudra would be dealt with firmly and there were reported cases of actions against those guilty of it. There was a bit of scare tossed up in the air and the political conditions were changing.

Dalits were now going to the schools, tramping feet in the temples, going about the markets, wearing fashionable dresses and the transition seemed on cards. The emergence of Bahujan Samaj Party and Rastriya Janta Dal in uttar Pradesh and Bihar lent credence to the slogan of social justice. The likes of Ambedkar and Ram Manohar Lohiya were revisited. The dragon of reservation raised its ugly head and the upper crest was pushed to the backwaters. The era of social justice was descending, rehabilitation of the dislodged, and the abrupt end of the feudal structure all was dispatched disdainfully to the dustbin of history. The Dalits were donning political colours, ushering in a new season of optimism, staking their share in just about everything. Nisith Narayan, the panditji was squatting outside the house with a bunch of Brahmins and talking of the resurgent Dalits. Ramdeo Pujari was almost ballistic for his angst against the rising audacity of the Dalits was unbearable for him. Nisith Babu, this Mahua, came to me the other day and do you know I could not recognize him. He was clad in a pair of jeans and a white tea shirt. Wow, what a scene it was, panditji, it left me stunned and he did not bother even to see me. He kept coming to me right until the entry point of my house and you know I had to stop him there otherwise he would have crept into my house and spoiled everything. That bastard Mahua, sala Harami, Madar... was combing his hair right before me. Nisith Babu wanted to intervene but he barely did it we must do something to put him back into his shoes but Nisith Babu seemed disinterested for he knew the times have changed and any action against him would mean trouble. He ignored all that was said by Ramdeo Pujari.

Rashmi was going upset for days together though she could not say anything to her father but deep down she was furious. Her angst was boiling though the admission to the B.Ed course was completed. She took the entrance test and cleared it. Bindu being a scheduled tribe was exempted from the entrance test and this was something that further agonized

Rashmi. The same day Shambunath came in the evening with a packet of sweets. He was very upbeat since his daughter Bindu was admitted to the B.Ed course. He was at the doorstep; Rashmi saw him and ignored him there only. He thought Rashmi would come forward to accept the packet of sweets but she went her own way. He thumped the door to which Nisith Narayan himself came out and gleefully accepted the packet and asked him to come in. It is very good that Rashmi and Bindu will be going together and remember this course is job oriented and they will get the jobs after the course comes to an end. Rashmi listened to all these and felt like crying. She muttered to herself I will not go with that Harijan. My God, this Baba does not understand anything. How to move with a Shudra, no, no, I think this would be too much. I do not want to spoil myself. She is a bloody outcast. This government is going mad and I have to be within my senses. The sound of the motorbike drew everybody's attention and it was the same Mahua with his new motorcycle. Shambunath was his uncle. Having seen Mahua, Shambunath chuckled a bit and told Nisith Babu, This Mahua is my nephew and gets five hundred rupees per month from the government for education as economic assistance. He came out of the house, sat behind Mahua on the Motorcycle, and looked back smilingly. From the other side Ramdeo Pujari emerged. A charred Ramdeo Pujari, Salaa….., look what is going on. This government has made our life hell. The man until yeaterday used to be sitting outside my house for some left over food and see, see, this Madar……. on a bike and see that Harami, Shambunath, how he is smiling. Sala Shudra ka Jana, Bahan……

Nisith Babu stood there having watched the whole drama and looked into the fuming eyes of Ramdeo Pujari. Ramdeo, what is wrong? You seem very upset. I cannot see that Mahua and these bloody shudras losing senses and it is because of this reservation and the soft-pedalling of the government. They are going overboard. I had asked Ramdas yesterday to do the bore well but do you know what he says? No, No, Nisith Babu intervened moved his head, come on Ramdeo Pujari, What you have not been able to appreciate is the support of the government and the policy of the vote bank. Remember this is a democracy, you cannot discriminate against anybody, the Shudras are now the ready vote bank for Lalooji, and the Muslims are rallying behind him since they have lost faith in Congress. Look, at this Dumrisarai, which has a good Muslim and Shudra population and Lalooji has kept coming to this village. The roads are under construction, electricity is improving, hospitals being given a facelift and the doctors who never bothered, now have to come to this hospital. You know how many doctors have been suspended for the dereliction of duty of late. Ramdeo Pujari, had the patience to endure whatever was said by Nisith Babu but he wanted to know as why this Mahua and Ramdas are not abiding. That is because they think that no longer they can be coerced into anything against their will. In addition, they are getting the funds from the government. Therefore, they have nothing to worry. Jobs are reserved, admission to all colleges are reserved, of course a certain percentage. Then why should now be at your door begging for things. The long introductory address of Nisith Babu came to a halt only when Rashmi emerged with cups of tea. Ramdeo, take this tea and the problem with you is that you tend to be oblivious of the political changes sweeping the state. You are a very emotional fellow.

Rashmi thought it is the best time for her to leave her standpoint on the issue of going with Bindu to the college. Also the presence of Ramdeo Pujari gave her some additional support. Bab.. Babaaa. She fumbled initially but still resolute to make her point. Yes, Bitiya, is there anything you want to say. Babaa, I will not go to the college with Bindu. No, I cannot go with her. She hardly completed her sentence; the dramatic reaction of Ramdeo Pujari was interesting. What Bitiya. That, Bindu, the daughter of Shambunath. Nisith Babu, are you completely bereft of the basic sense or are you hell-bent to lose whatever sanctity of your sanctified status remains. That shudra, salaa shambhuaa...

I don't know how he coughed up the audacity to ask you to send his daughter with yours. What has made you do this? I think, hell is coming live to this earth and what else remains for us. I would love to die before doing it. Bitiya will have to endure the humiliation of going with that Bindu. Where is shambhua ... Madar... I am just going to him to ask whether he can really do it. Nisith Babu was all aghast at the stubborn stance of Ramdeo Pujari and he knew he is a temperamental man and can do anything. He persuaded him to stay cool and he just suggested whether it could be a possibility. He looked towards his daughter and there was a bit of fire in his eyes. Rashmi you just go inside. You people make a mountain out of a hole. Ramdeo Pujari stood to leave but Nisith Babu knew the man is still hot and he might do things that can be a problem for all. Arre, Ramdeo, I never said that Rashmi would be going with her, all I suggested was a possible movement together since the College is a bit far from here and the two girls can be together for each other's company. I did not know there would be a reaction of the kind Rashmi has shown. Ok, I will find some way out. He pacified the situation in his own way and to an extent nullified the fire Ramdeo Pujari's eyes were oozing out. An uneasy silence hung there and Ramdeo still was unrelenting. Nisith Babu stood up and looked back to find somebody as the footsteps drew closer. It was Jassu Thakral. Jassu, where were you all these days. You disappear like anything. Ramdeo Pujari did not like the presence of Jassu Thakral. Bhai, these days small shoes are looking for big sizes and the wind of politics is not leaving anybody untouched. May be he went to the town to try his fortune. So when you would be fighting elections. Ramdeo quipped in a more teasing style. Jassu knew Ramdeo is having a dig at him but he kept his cool. Shudra fellows are not with you today. He commented further. Jassu now shot back. Ramdeoji, feudal lordship is now a reverie, get out of the utopian world and see the reality for yourself. There was a bit of sarcasm involved in his remarks passed to further entice Ramdeo Pujari. Now Ramdeo lost his cool, Saala, Jassu, Massu, what do you think, you can be the leader of the Harijans, another incarnation of Gandhi, bloody hell, you just count the number of pieces you will go into and if I am checking myself it is for the Nisith Babu only. Or else I would have ripped and broken you like woods. Saala, bastard, leadership is telling on him. Remember, a handful of Shudras cannot win you the elections. We are also the voters you are discounting. The heated exchange left the two very sore. Ramdeo Pujari, almost pushed Jassu and walked away in rage.

Jassu Thakral was busy building his local influence. He started meeting people, attending social gatherings and visiting slums and the hamlets largely inhabited by the shudras and the backwards. He identified himself as one of them singing and humming the same songs. He was desperately trying to make some inroads into their psyche as one advocate of their cause and convincing them that if he is given the support, he would do everything possible for the better quality of their life. The elections were announced and the time left was not much. He ran to city every now and then, camped in blocks for days together, mobilized the local lads, garnered funds and received some from the party. He had the blessings of the top brass of the state leadership. He was a busy man. He was also seen moving with a bunch of Muslim lads and the caste equation though not on his side but he worked out his own permutations and counted the support of the Shudras and the Muslims. The Muslim voters were perhaps not very clear about the selection of the candidate but Jassu had mingled so much with them that it was just a matter of a decision. The other day when Shubrati Miyan's son had frallen sick all of a sudden, Jassu took him to the hospital in the city and did everything for him. The money for treatment was also given to him. Since then Shubrati Mian is all for him. The Jolaha vote was bound to fall in his kitty. In addition, the other Muslim segments had an inclination for the Lantern, the symbol of Laloo's party. The Brahmins had no choice but to support Ramesh Kushwaha of the JDU. Laloo, Paswan, Kanchan Singh, Pappu Yadav all visited the Dumrisarai village to take stock of the political situation. Ramdeo Pujari was working hand for Ramesh Kushwaha but he did not seem to do much to cut into the votes of Jassu Thakral. Nisith Babu had no interest in the elections but it was Ramdeo who took him to the dusty roads of Dumrisarai for the canvassing in favour of Ramesh Kushwaha. Nisith Babu talked to the people of his own community and somewhat was despaired to see the lack of enthusiasm on the part of his caste for they believed that Jassu was a better bet but they had their own reasons not to support him. Ramdeo Pujari, just a day before the elections collected about a dozen lumpens from his community and attacked the house of some Shudras just outside the village. The news spread like a wild fire. He wanted to malign Jassu right on the eve of the elections to leave a message that Jassu is backstabbing and the attack infact was engineered by jassu only. The police arrested Ramdeo Pujari a day before the election. He was put behind the bar accused of attacking the Harijans.

Elections were held on the given date. Jassu was quite upbeat and he knew he is there in the reckoning. His optimism was not misplaced. The election results were announced after a week and the verdict went in favour of Jassu Thakral. Ramdeo Pujari though released from the custody was a sore individual but still he was much the same man. He called Jassu, the re-incarnate of Shudras. Jassu ignored all his prejudices in the euphoria of his victory.

# A Wet Morning

The midnight rain left the morning wet. It was all wet. The sky still displayed deep and stark patches of clouds and the threat of another spell of rain seemed realistic. Last night was the tale wrapped in a bit of horror. The sky was in its elements. The thunderbolts produced intimidating sounds, very akin to an explosion on earth that is tempered with the excesses of human imagination. Science went to the moon reducing the art of living to a crisis. All these permeated an exasperated mind. Amritraj, was a little out of sorts and all these thoughts wreaked havoc and pushed him into a spot. He seemed to realize and remember the words of Shakuntala, yes the same Shakuntala, who met him on the Hamdaan Street. She was electrifying in her strides, brown eyes with deep marks of cuts above her eyelid. He could still think how she came right behind him and stood for a while. He did not observe it until the pat on his back had awakened him to the reality of the moment. She was clad in a purple top with black trousers. The height was good, a pair of lanky legs though not staggering, she held her ground exuding good confidence. Amritraj could feel she was young, into a shady business somewhat but still thoroughly unsure of what she exactly wanted from him. She left just a word, "Shakuntala, I will see you later." He perhaps wanted to know as why she was behind him and when the rains picked up rage, she opened her umbrella, took a cab and disappeared in a huff. When he came back to his room, he did not remember anything for a place like Abu Dhabi, these kinds of encounters were routine affairs. He did not want to go into it but still he did not forget it all. He went past the Naser Square, past the same Hamdaan Street and unconsciously held on there trying to find the same woman. He stood there motionless, looking rather quizzically. His steps were rooted there. One, two, three, four minutes, now it was more than ten minutes, he did not move. The glossy cars, painted and perfumed women, young and the old seemed running to their directions. He was also getting late but he didn't know the motive of his stay there. Looked at the watch and it warned him of the delay. He again put his legs in motion, looking back at regular intervals as if he was waiting for a call from behind. Nothing happened. He was bare, his mind was bare, stripped of all thoughts and kept going. At office, he was not the same man, not the ebullient self, tea, coffee, cigarette all waited for him. He whisked out one from the pack of twenty, lighted it and took a deep and long puff. The billowing smoke blurred his vision, he wanted his vision to be blurred, and his memory tormented him. He left his chair, walked up and down, looked down the balcony. All was quiet. He too was very quiet. Cars ran, pedestrians lifted their heavy feet, slim girls whizzed past. It was eleven thirty. The clock tower right before him reminded him of the hour in the day. He turned and ensconced himself on the sofa. Comfortable, deep cushion gave him the velvet feel but he was not there.

The day at office was over. Throughout the day he did nothing. Everything was postponed for tomorrow. Everything was suspended for the day. He took long but heavy strides forward in a direction he thought, might lead him to another chance encounter with Shakuntala. Yes, Shakuntala was her name. She looked pretty sharp. A few seconds only, Amritraj rued his absence and the indifference he had at the most crucial time towards her. He could have at least seen her, talked to her and might have done something to know more about her. But why was he so concerned? The question came from within. He had no answer. Looked towards heaven as if seeking another go. Amritraj was a very soft spoken individual, a few words on anything and that was all. He was short of words. Also short of the reaction time. That's why he missed out on Shakuntala. He was not a chaser of girls either. He never did in his life though a listener of tales. Tales amused him of all hues and in those tales he sought the direction of his own life. He took his lunch half-heartedly. At office he avoided it. He cantered into his studio flat right behind the clock tower and in front of the huge fountain. He flung himself to the bed, closed his eyes and put to sleep. While the nap was almost on, the thud at the door made it disappear. Amritraj cuddled into the bed, hesitantly summoned the lost energy and went to the door at a short distance. He yawned before the door, lifted his left hand and opened the door latch. He still was in the throes of a half baked sleep. Sometime what you chase is just a step away, thought Amritraj. He could gather himself in the wake of a visit made by somebody who interfered with just about everything he did since he met her last. I am Shakun...tala, the second part was completed by Amritraj. Can I come in and so sorry to disturb you. Amritraj did not know how to react; rather he showed her the way to the hall. Shakuntala went to the corner of a seat in the hall and Amritraj still under the spell of an incredible situation took a seat away from her. Shakuntala's perfume rendered the atmosphere heavy.

Do you live alone? Came the query breaking the settling silence. Yes. Three lettered word was enough he thought to answer her query.

I saw you the other day at the Hamdaan Street but the rains came hard and I had to leave. I saw you in the morning also. Perhaps you were going to your office. Where do you work? Amritraj almost whispered. Tebodino, a Dutch firm. A finance officer. Wow.

You are an Indian; the question was banged again upon him while its second part was held back. Which part? Gujarat, Ahmedabad. I am from Banglore and this is my sixth year here. I work with a consultancy. How many years have you completed here? The same, Amritraj made it very short. Meanwhile Shakuntala stood up, and took a stroll round the corner. She looked at just about everything, she moved into the room, kitchen, everywhere she found space. Nice flat, well in order. To find a bachelor with a sense of order is really astonishing. Are you married? No, Amritraj could sense the informal ways of Shakuntala. Would you like to have coffee or tea? She was forthright. Tea. Amritraj moved into the kitchen for tea. He re-emerged soon with the same tea and Shakuntala picked her cup soon. Sipping tea and looking around, continued in the same flair, I live very close to you that is on the other side of the clock tower. I wanted to know something about you and I thought it best to come to you than to make you come to any other point. Amritraj was left dazed, almost infuriated, for he could see the relative ease Shakuntala had displayed throughout. There was no nervousness, no hesitation; she was cool as cucumber and cold as ice. He admired the confidence of the lady, still thinking as what might have been the motive to visit a stranger like him and talk with an astounding measure of confidence. He was wondering only to be intercepted by Shakuntala's voice, can I take leave now. She stood up abruptly and proceeded to the door, but all of a sudden held on, looked back, came close to him, offered her hand. She shook his hand and left.

Amritraj was a blend of delight and surprise. His eyes kept chasing her throughout the day, he hopped from places to places, and squatted at the points he would have never liked but never thought that she would come to him the way she did. She was young. Perhaps she was voluptuous too. She appeared like a bright morning. Amritraj started going wild but soon arrested the astray movement of thoughts. But one thing was there. She said nothing, expressed nothing. She came, she saw and she left. Was it enough to conquer him? The man within him was awakened for a while.

It was Thursday. Amritraj got up late as it was a usual habit with him to be in the bed for late hours on Thursdays for it was a day of break from the breakneck pace. His cell blared. He does not talk much on cell for he does not like it and his people know it very well. But still on Thursday the cell ringing was not a common situation for him. He avoided it. The first call went unheeded. The cell again blared. He was furious, come on I don't like this and picked the phone with a louder hello. Hello. Hello. Is it Amritraj? He hung on to his silence. Amritraj, its Shakuntala. Yeah. Amritraj. It again kept it very simple. I know you are at home. In the next half an hour you will get my next call and by that time I think you should be ready. We are going out for lunch. It left him confused. No request, nothing like that. It was an order, Amritraj thought it to be just an order against which he had no defence. But there was no protest.

He got the call on the expected time and he hurried his steps to see Shakuntala. As he moved out, he found the same bright morning, clad in a blue top against a pair of black trousers. She appeared impeccable from a distance. Both joined each other in the corridors of fancy. No word was uttered.

Amritraj was very happy that day. Perhaps for the first time, perhaps he does not remember when he was happy last time. He was full of energy, the song of life was sung with his own concealed self and the music it produced left nothing for him to long for. He was gay and jocund. Meetings with Shakuntala continued on weekends. Month one, two and a host of it went by and he did not know how old the relationship was. They held hands, kissed each other, looked deep into the eyes, wore the best they had, ate to the satisfaction. All was hunky-dory. Gradually, relationship went beyond the formulated phrase and each day was a day of song and dance. An individual like Amritraj knew little about the nitty-gritty of the human complexities.

A year later, Amritraj was in his own flat, the same Thursday it was. He was waiting for both Shakuntala and her call. There was a knock at the door. Amritraj lost no time and ran towards the door. Opened it hastily only to be tossed up in a clink. The police force it was. Yes the cops and the constables. What is this? He fumbled for words. Fuming at the spectacle, he cried, what you want. The cops barged into his flat. Arrested him; the shout of the police officer crashed his world. He could not ask why he was arrested once he came to know that Shakuntala had relations with the underworld. He smiled, very happy to be arrested if it was for her bright morning, Shakuntala. He cried in agonizing pain. Shakuntala ... Shakuntala ...

# An Encounter at Noon

Mohandas was all desires, a bundle of desires and he did not ever bother the life he lived and the direction it had strayed into. He was a happy go lucky man, reaping the benefits of all that accrued from the will left by his own father. Women, wine, luxury, extravagance were the things that constituted the menu of his existence. Like all nights that night when there was a blast just outside the hotel he was putting up, he gave a damn to it but the girl wanted to go, obviously perturbed by the intimidating explosion but Mohandas was unrelenting and he clutched her even more firmly. An altercation followed and the girl was almost strangulated. The cries of the girl made the hotel security run to the room number 502. It was opened after a long persuasion and the girl was found lying on the ground, bare and unconscious. Mohandas was shivering and shuddering. He took the manager of the hotel in confidence and paid some money to get the issue thrashed out. The girl survived the attack but vowed to strike back at a man who never knew the emotions and feelings. For him a girl was a bare body with bare flesh on it. After the explosion, investigations began and every room was examined with all details. One of the occupants was Mohandas. His room number was taken note of because a nervous manager did take his name as a suspect. Details of him were hunted and the next day he was picked up for interrogation. While the interrogation was on Mohandas showed signs of nervousness as there were some tricky questions raised by the interrogation team and he having no good reason to be there in the hotel found himself falling into the trap. Throughout the interrogation, Mohandas was jittery and every question made him lose his ground. He was released after the interrogation but permission to leave the station was not granted. He was advised to report to the police station every other day. For a man like Mohandas who did not look beyond the bottles of whiskey and wine and women and the body, this was a rigorous exercise for him and it spoiled his carefree life.

It was the time for Mohandas to turn to the wine as darkness had dropped itself, there was a bit of murky light heaping the tattered shop situated behind the hut. Mohandas knew he could find some wine there. As he advanced rapidly towards the liquor shop, he almost ran into a girl. It was almost dark for the lamp overhead burning was too fragile and most of the people had gone back to their homes since the sensation was still reigning supreme and the rumour mill was in full cry. The girl recovered quickly, stared dangerously at Mohandas who did not seem to realize it, and hurriedly ran towards the shop. The girl followed him. As soon he turned away from the shop, Mohandas found a shadow right behind almost chasing him. Since the urgency of wine was playing havoc, he did not take any notice but the girl kept following him. He was about to get into a cheap hotel as all the big hotels were given his name for not providing any accommodation to him, he being blacklisted. The girl uncovered her face, forced herself in and once the light was switched on, she could see who the man was. Mohandas too went red to see the same girl who, he thought is responsible for most of his troubles. You bitch, a whore and rogue, a leftover of thousand men, get the hell out of here. He shouted and turned furious. What are you doing here? I know you and the likes of you. You stretch your legs only to squeeze money from wealthy people. You fucking cunt, get lost. The girl was quiet and went through the vituperative outbursts of Mohandas very comfortably as if he was heaping adulations on her. After Mohandas had collapsed to the chair, his forehead dipped in sweat, the girl advanced towards him and asked him to cool down because the situation outside was very explosive. Mohandas did not want further troubles and resigned to her advice. The girl introduced herself as Rohini though Mohandas was confident that she had a different name in the hotel "Cool breeze." But he did not say anything. Rohini expressed her desire to be with him for the night. Mohandas was quickly reminded of his needs at night and he thanked God for the same.

The morning was lacking the spirit it generally has and the sense of heaviness was all pervasive. Mohandas cuddled into his bed, threw his hands about to find Rohini but the velvet feel of the human body was replaced by a hard touch of the bed. He quickly got up and muttered to his own self, oh, no, where the bitch has disappeared. He came out of the room, out of the hotel, looking around, chasing as much distance as it was possible for him. Nevertheless, she was just not there. He found himself completely out of gear and his mind turned into a cobweb of doubts. Where she had gone, what possibly was her plans and whether she has connections with the police? For a moment he thought, the police Jeep is right behind him. He looked back desperately and heaved a sigh of relief. He came back to his room fuming and sputtering, did not know what to do. He could not go out too far since he was himself under surveillance. His cell blared, a call from Bhai, oh no what the hell it is. Nothing seems to be right for him. Bhai, what a burdensome thought it was for him. He had no choice but to attend to the call. He picked the phone being too scared, and a hesitant Bhai. Yes Bhai. On the other end the commanding officer made his breath hold on for a while, Mohandas, the voice was hard and rough, yes Bhai. Rohini was there last night with you. Yes, Bhai. She was here with me. Do you know why? No Bhai, I don't know because you are not complying with the orders. Just a minor blast in a city like Ratnagiri and you think you have done your job. Don't forget the police still suspects you and you just might be in trouble. Listen carefully Mohandas, what you have to do next. Yes Bhai, I am listening. Sweat permeated all parts of his body. Yes, Bhai, carry on, I am here. You have no choice and any lapse on your part can mean what, do you know, you going into pieces. So listen carefully. At 3.30 Rohini will meet you outside the Coolbreeze hotel and there she will hand you over a list of instructions and some important addresses. Please be careful and be on your guard. I need faultless execution. Details will be from Rohini. Remember 3.30 pm. The phone was disconnected. Mohandas was in shreds, he rued his relationship with the Bhais. He questioned himself as what was the need to be in their dragnet. Ok, they did help him in getting the will of his foster father implemented through the court orders and the court knew that he himself was the murderer of his father but the Bhais wielded their clout to get him the will going. Though Mohandas had already paid a good price for it but that was not enough for them. He was now a puppet and they have held his breath hostage. He thought he was better off without the will and without the money. He killed his foster father by pushing him under a speeding truck on the highways. Yes, he is a criminal and he must suffer, he must pay for his sins. He was convinced and consoled himself that he has the expertise to execute things and he reassured that he can trust his skills. At 3 O' clock, he set out for the envisaged destination. Rohini was right there. He gave a frowning look to the bitch and snatched the papers from her hand. Rohini was all smiles and quipped there only. I slept with you last night in that dingy lodge and you bastard did all that you could have done to a woman. Now see, this is the premium that you have to pay. She wore a diabolic smile that suggested the victory of a humbled woman. Mohandas's teeth stuttered and blanched with frustration but there was nothing he could do. His looks reminded the portrait of a fallen and defeated soldier. Rohini, walked away from there, having pushed him in a total mess.

Mohandas regrouped himself and induced the lost confidence in his ability to carry out big operations. He did one in Maharashtra, one in Gujarat and one in Rajasthan with exemplary courage and boldness. Fear does not strike him as he was a merciless merchant of death. He came back to his room without reading the instructions. Uncorked the bottle of whiskey and consumed the whole bottle in a single go. Now he was much relaxed, he lost his nervousness and came back to his deadly self. His eyes started oozing all fire and his body was burning with ire. He opened the paper and scanned the instructions given.

12.05. Target. Ahmadnagar.
Nature of blast. RDX.
Expected casualty. 300 people.
Time of execution. 11 am.
Day. Friday.

Ammunition to be collected from Pirzada Mohammad at Ahmadnagar.

Mohandas read the instructions with complete composure and wore a devilish smile on his lips just the way a butcher smiles before guillotining the animals. He dressed himself in black, put on the gloves at about 9.30 am and drove to Ahmadnagar in Tata Sumo. Wearing dark glasses, he at times peered through the vehicle without being jittery and showed no signs of nervousness. He seemed to be an accomplished doer and a master of human doom. He found Pirzada Mohammad on the outskirts of Ahmadnagar. He raised his hands and Pirzada collected a packet from the tea stall on the other side of the road and handed it over to Mohandas. He exchanged just a hello and left. Pirzada had scattered beard on his face, dressed to perfection, tall, good looking and created a deceptive aura of a man. That perhaps sufficed to escape the public glare. Mohandas took Tata Sumo close to the tea stall, removed his glasses and ordered for a cup of tea. Sat there with the people, shared the discussion on the local issues with them as if he was one of them. He checked time. Just an hour to go before Ahmadnagar turns into a graveyard. All seemed in line and the dice was spruced up for a massive destruction. Mohandas kept his eyes on the watch. Still there was sometime to go. He stood there waiting for the zero hour. As he stood there, he saw Pirzada running wildly.

Some people had already gathered there while he kept running. He had shouted at the top of his voice, police, police, somebody has done it. Mohandas got the message, as he turned to get into his Tata Sumo, a police van blocked his way leaving no space for him to do anything with his vehicle. Sensing the trouble, he took to his heels, whisked the loaded pistol and fired in the air to cast a spell of horror on the people around but the police force had already cordoned off the whole area. He ran into a bush to hide himself but the police inspector saw him and moved into the same direction. He fired on him, the police inspector fired back. Rounds of bullets were exchanged. Mohandas was hit on his shoulders and he bled profusely. However, he was unrelenting. He kept firing blindly but his bullets were all fired in panic, self-defence and exasperation. The police force advanced towards the bush and fired many rounds while inching forward. The police inspector Ahmad Hussain was a brave man. Undeterred by the onrushing bullets, he kept his cool and from a close range pumped as many bullets he could have that riddled Mohandas's body. He was dead lying in a pool of blood. Pirzada also could not escape. The two bodies were kept for the public display. People were patting the back of the police inspector Ahmad Hussain for his heroics. Both Pirzada and Mohandas breathed their last.

# Breaking House

The sky seemed more than blue; the radiance about it, spoke at length the poverty of his thoughts. A little confused, Rishi, sat on the sofa close to the bed, the crackling sound of water rushing from the old fountain behind the balcony tampered with the harmony of the moment, the apparent resignation to the unseen troubles knocking at the door, only to be seen by him, to be read by him, left him a little harried. The smoke of cigarette covered his face, the fingers the cigarette was tucked between flickered and the ash fell on the ground to be swept away by his feet. The glass of water half filled, the marks of lipstick on it still glowing like a half moonlit night, the streak of light creeping in rather hesitantly did not impress him. Still not in the best of dispositions, not in the worst of crisis, he meandered towards the balcony to strike a response with the outside world. It was the same old day, the sun blazed down as it does; the houses appeared like a set of matchboxes, the bare terraces, the tin roofs, the unspeakable sound of the summer heat, all seemed burning with rising temperature, the boxes of the air conditioners, its back pushed out like a hefty woman bending its back and drops of water plummeting to the ground, hot as hell, like fire at its burning best.

The time gave the impression that it is not looking back, Rishi could think barely of the last few days spent or squandered away, whether there was any construction involved or any meaningful thought permeated his mind. It was bare, the mind was not without its own share of apprehension, and the thoughts all ran away, spewed contempt for him. The city seemed too sedate, the lull presided over the hearts, the dripping boredom, the birds going quiet, the kids deserting streets, the oldies sulking in shrivelling sockets, the sound of the vehicles staggered to mess about and meddle into the reigning silence.

All that he wanted to recall did not leave any imprint and remained locked in a state of restlessness. Nishi had left with her father after that fateful day. What she might have thought, whether good or bad he had nothing to do with it.

It was all arrogance, elitism at its torturous best. What if she had stayed back, thought about the tension, the mounting wedge, the relationships, a host of it whether hers or mine, all are part of the same society she lives in, I live in. She was not my choice, Rishi's monologue continued, the wedding night, the successive nights after, the following days, months, years all were like speechless moments, mute moments, moments mired in unspeakable chaos, taciturn time. But what the fault was? Whose fault? His mind reeled backwards, refused space to the thoughts for Nishi. No, she was not fair, not just the kind of girl who would ever care for the rights of men, the rights of women, the rights of all. No, she was an individual, just one individual, with a lot of things within. What she wanted, the thing she valued, her mother, her father lived separately, lived their privacy in the prime of youth, and parted ways when the sanction sought by a defining society was refused. The daughter of the same parents grew with fashionable ideas, ideas in conflict with the double faced society. Call it elite culture; call it the ultra learned society with its own system of relationship. Nishi might have been influenced by the very life her parents lived, the very culture they created and the very definitions of free life.

What is free life, he wondered? Rishi's mind was now tired, done in by the spate of thoughts, all were uncomfortable. These three years with Nishi were all about finding new concepts of culture, relationship, values, moral code and ethics. Just before she left, she had told him that Rikki is her friend for some years. What bewildered him more was the presence of Rikki in his own house in his absence and even while he was around, it made no difference for the two. They would giggle much the same way, the song and dance, the music player, the jokes and jests and Nishi time and again hugging Rikki in an inebriated state. Alcohol, bottles of it would litter the ground, the scantily clad Nishi speaking incoherent language left him thinking whether Nishi was his wife or a hired woman. He could hardly question her and whenever he did it the reaction that Nishi produced was disturbing. "This is the problem of the middle class, you people cannot look beyond a woman as an object, and you cannot realize or ever understand that there is something more than what you think.This is relationship, friendship and the life, perhaps you will not understand."

That evening Rikki came in a glossy car, blared horn, Nishi clad in a black top that went up the waist, caprie exposed her sheen right up to the thighs, eyelashes crammed the space for anything there while he stood outside the house watching with utter pain his wife going away with a friend. He could barely move his eyes wrapped in pain, thought to stop her but was again reminded of the cliché that had been a part of his conjugal existence, we are just friends. Night clubs, parties, discotheque, men of all hues dancing, singing, hugging, kissing, all in the name of friendship. Rishi thought, what on earth her parents chose him for her, only to make his life miserable, only to make him realize what elite culture represents. Rishi had no choice since his father had already agreed.

He would often call his father and report all about Nishi's wild lifestyle, her adventures, her open relationship, her disdainful disregard for the family values and his father would just advise him to be patient for she belongs to the high ups and he is reading too much into it. Rishi was suffocated almost to death, he lost his sleep, the bouts of depression were more intermittent, and the domestic violence seemed round the corner.

The evening drew closer, shadows draped; the birds were returning to the nests, the sound of cuckoo left a soothing impact but Rishi was equally restless. He wanted to resolve the issue once and for all. He had been burning, enraged, fuming for Nishi had been away for the last eight hours. The sons of capitalism were making bestial dance over the proletariat streets, over the conscience of the dignified individuals, over the self respect of the upright souls, over the subdued rage of the voiceless and over the decorum of value loving society. Nishi sunk in the glory of the hour made her way back to the house. She seemed sapped of all energy, her lips had dried up, her top was rumpled, her eyelashes had disappeared and she formed an image of a woman abandoned by the arrogance of opulence. Rishi had made a decision to get out of the rut, out of the daily dreary suffocation, out of the deadly and dastardly acts of tolerance.

Nishi cantered back to her room, threw herself to the bed and the half spoken words like Rikki, what a soul.... You......are... my .... Life.....my......love.....my ... my....all....that......

Rishi was more than saddened by whatever was uttered by his own wife, hung on there, stood bare minded, face turned into a red blob of meat, hands were trembling and the ire of a husband was waiting to find its moment of expression.

The morning breeze had its quota of heat, the sun blazed down as fiercely as it could; the sky was bereft of all ideas while Rikki on that morning had all the resources in the world to strike back.

By 10.30 Nishi recovered her senses and asked for lemon water. Rishi,was rooted to the ground and told her to wait. After a while he just bumped into the room with a thud.

Where were you the whole day yesterday? The question had a tinge of fire? What do you mean? You know it was Rikki's birthday party.

That bastard.
Nishi sprung from her bed as if an electric current had been passed through her body.
Are you crazy?
Yes. Where is that capitalist bastard who sucks the blood of young wives, girls and vamps like you?
Nishi in fact was still not sure of what struck her ears.
Nishi, where you are man? The likes of you lick his dust and live on his waste.
Yes the likes of you who sell her body for the heck of parties and bucks that he must be stuffing in your cleavages.
Mind your language, Nishi lost her cool and warned Rishi.
Come on bitch, you are a slur on womanhood itself. This is what your mother did, this is what your father did and this is what your... whole c .l..a..n......did.

Things hotted up to the unmanageable extent and Rishi was more than certain to polish off the tails of relationship to usher in a new era of peace for himself.

Rishi, what do you think, you are an officer, a first class officer but remember, Rikki dashes off officers like you every day and if I make call to him now then I do not know what would be your condition... and ......
How shameless a bitch you are, Rishi retorted.
Elite, yes your father was elite, your mother was elite and now you are an elite and I have seen how elitism defines itself. You little bitch and a thunderous sound crashed against the air. It was a heavy slap slanted on the right cheek of Nishi.

She grimaced in pain. Rishi, in the last three years had seen enough of the elitism, the ways of elitism, the culture it had created for itself and how the wives lunged forward on the besmirched streets.
He unleashed two more powerful slaps on the cheeks of Nishi and asked her to get out. Just get the hell out of here. You whore......

Nishi could hardly realize that Rishi who never spoke a word to her about her amorous adventures would finally have the courage to dismiss her from his life.

Nishi left with her father and Rikki sat on the balcony with the confidence of a man having achieved the lost manly features. He thought Nishi and her likes are the products of a particular culture and it is the same double faced society at the root of it. His mind wandered to the thoughts of Zarina. What a graceful girl she was, but it is religion, the caste, the other flimsy affiliations that stop the society from its own purgation.

# Boot Polish

They twittered like birds, spoke to each other without reservations and promised all bonhomie. They were like a pair of frogs lolloping together, singing the same tune of drudgery, complacency and despair. All was done in tandem. They knew very little, there was no drive either to know more for they asked no questions, nothing disconcerting and kept their desires close to their hearts. Ragini and Sursatia were two individuals in the circus of life, living it without the ho-ha and without making any song and dance about it. Both were tender with tender sensations, eyes ran a certain distance and beyond it was all darkness. Deep and stark darkness. Ragini, a modest girl from a modest background, too modest infact a background to make any mention of it. She was heaped upon the choicest abuses from the morning to the setting of the sun. Early rising ensured tougher existence for the day and the same day would become too long for her. Broom, bucket, scrubbers were her apparatus, day to day apparatus with which she swept away the adverse currents of life, the apparatus that gave her the confidence of her own being, that reminded her the heartbeat of a living individual. Her father, Mangra Ram, was all bones pieced together; breath seemed oscillating between the nose and lips, a gippy stomach with a huge appetite. Hunger introduced itself from a distance, eyes struggled to recollect the lost vision but the tongue wagged eloquently. Locally made spurious liquor was his lifeblood and it gave him the reason to exist, to live the haggard existence. He returns late in the night with his friends, Sangru, Budhia, Kisna, Shubrati, Ramjani and Radhey singing the broken songs of life, taking steps though hesitant together having spent all that was garnered through the day. At home, Ragini would be at the receiving end facing the ire of the lost consciousness. Saali, Randi, the (fucking bitch) stuffs her money in her...... He would use all his strength to rip her trouser cord to unearth the money he, thinks, she keeps there. A bewildered Ragini, would do her best to ward off the threat that seemed more than realistic.

Sursatia, a very tall girl, whitish and slightly dark complexion, nose straight as stick, squint eyes squirming alarmingly sat on her features. She too had the same tale, of the indifference heaped by the nature on her as her mother left very early and her uncle raised her. The only good thing was the benign presence of her father, Rambali Das, who like Mangra Ram, was wedded to liquor. Living in a broken hamlet with Aunt who was as bad a woman as anyone from her gender could be. Everyday was a new beginning in terms of the travails of life. Chamartoli, a microcosmic universe had all the ingredients of the theatre of the absurd, where life was like a shrinking sun, a real bedlam throughout the day and night and so full of screeching sounds travelling quite a distance. Sangru, Budhia, Kisna, Mangru, Rambali, Jhabru, Sohni, Ramkali, Bindiya, Shyamli, and the likes of these lived life amid the descending shadows of gloom and the shadows kept creeping up all the time. Early morning huge sounds of male and female voices would surround all human ears and the movements of the elements like Mangru and Sangru made it look so different from any other locality in town. The somewhat saner element was Jhabru Chamar, who did not show any urgency to either abuse his kids and wife or do any nonsense, which could have drawn the attention of the dwellers of Chamartoli. He would sedately walk past the people engaged in scuffle or altercation or making some unpalatable gestures but he would hardly bother for all these. His profession was demanding, for he used to have long days sewing, polishing shoes while sitting outside the pavement of a shop. He was very popular particularly among those customers who were old and kept coming to him for a long time. They were his pet customers who would come to him and even help him when he needed most. A bidi tucked between the lips, smoke enveloping his face was his casual look, waiting for customers with hope in eyes and a graceful smile. His look was at times haggard, hair though some stood erected, a moustache that curled up at times and the potholes on the face made him look shabby. Clad in a stained shirt sitting on his haunches, reasonably adept in the art of saluting. Muslim customers were greeted with a salam and for the Hindus a warm namaste would appear on his carved lips and the same graceful smile as if he was inviting them to a reception. His operational area was Patna Market, dominated by the Muslims and he had been occupying that place for the last twenty years, so in a way he had seen that Patna Market rising from the ashes. He was the boss there and those who lined up with him respected him. They would accept customers only when Jhabru gave his nod though Jhabru never bothered for the customers. Local politics, the shooting prices, the changing culture of the city, girls reducing clothes all concerned him and he would discuss very intensely all these with his customers. Hands would run on the shoes with a breakneck pace with cherry polish, taking off the remains of the dirt on it with a busy tongue. He was a very good advisor to his customers. Bhaiya, this shoe is now in its final flickers and the coming rains likely to see through it. After that, I suspect there will not be much about it. The customer nodding head in agreement was a common sight. His customers were of all hues, rich, and poor, old, young and would boast to the fellow boot polishers that I have polished shoes that were introduced in the early part of the 1960 by Bata and what shoes they were, I reckon. Tea, he could gulp down with convenient ease and lots of tea throughout the day kept him on the wires of energy. He was short in height, eyes pushed inside the skull almost but he ran like an athlete, a lightweight body helped him do things on a good pace. Just beside him was Punditji's shop of the articles of the Hindu marriage like vermilion, garland with beads of flower studded in it and the religious towels encrypted with shlokas in Sanskrit.

That Punditji was hefty, tall, roving eyes, beetle juice dripping to the lips and the eyes kept vigil on the movement around.

Punditji was his close pal sharing the chuckles and the despair and all his grief Punditji knew. Someday, Jhabru would sit back home particularly during the rains cursing it and hoping for the sun to break through. At home he was the most uncomfortable man for he disliked Chamartoli thoroughly which he thought is a dangerous place to dwell in. His son, Mahi, ailed him and he found himself assailed and arraigned by his behaviour. Wandering all day long aimlessly around the Chamartoli with a bunch of lumpens, going over to the stagnant pool of water repeatedly and being there for hours together was a common activity for him. Chamartoli dwellers had a serious practical problem and that was of a toilet and bathroom. All men and women went outside for the natural calls. Women early in the morning while men though did not mingle with them but went to the other side of the open field. Jhabru found it very disconcerting and for years together, he had been trying to collect some money to construct a toilet but all his money that he could save, was frittered away by his son, Mahi. The stagnant pool was the most visited place by the local lads as there the young girls bathed in the day light and bared their chest to the feast of their eyes. Sohnia dangerously young and full blooded girl was the cynosure of all eyes and so were Ragini and Sursatia. They moved together to the stagnant pool and behind them was the bunch of boys led by Mahi. They knew that they are being followed and what for they knew that even better. The same evening Jhagru was approached by a host of elderly people with a catalogue of complaints against Mahi. Jhagru went up in flames for this was the first time he had to talk to the people he never thought he would in his lifetime. A thorough beating took place and Mahi was put under house arrest. Jhagru that night went to the bed early being fatigued and petrified over the deeds of his son. He was engaged in serious thoughts trying to find ways to get rid of his son who was beginning to be a trouble for him.

Jhagru had lost his wife sometime back and he rued her death most that night. Without mother, he thought, the son was going wild. He keeps out for the day, his daughter, Mohia runs his house in his absence but to tame Mahi is not her cup of tea. He thought and thought vigorously but all he faced was despair in the darkness of the night.

Next morning he tucked the boot tools under his arm and advanced slowly towards his daily destination, lost and visibly upset still exerting his mind to find a way to deal with his brat son. The sun was mild as the winter sun normally is and the brightness of the sun warmed his body a bit. He got into the Auto Rickshaw and soon found himself speeding away to the route he had been negotiating for the last twenty years. Every inch of the road, every nook and corner, every tea stall, every shop seemed to be a tale he was listening to, over a period. Things were so familiar. The roads that were deserted until yesterday were habited today and the colonies sprang up as if shrubs. There was a time that people were scared of venturing out after six in the evening and today things hot up at six. How quickly things have changed?. However, he was the same Jhagru in the last twenty years he saw people drawing from strength to strength but he found himself to the contrary reeling backwards with each passing day. The same space outside Khadi Udyog, the same Pandit with his shop, neither rising nor sinking, the same tools of boot polish, the same swirling crowd, perhaps he was a lost man in the crowd, he thought he was trying to recover himself from the crowd. All seemed on the move but the wheel of his life had too many spanners in it. It clogged his movement further. Chamartoli, the same wretched people like Mangru, Sangru, Shubrati, Radhey all stood before his eyes like a bad dream. The Auto Rickshaw came to an abrupt halt. Jhagru was unmoved. The driver shouted Jhagru. Jhagru, and there was nothing Jhgaru could do to move himself. He was squatted on the back seat with his breath having been switched away. He did not know when. Perhaps nobody noticed his breath deserting his body.

# Romancing in Clouds

The evening lurked, the shadows lengthened the chirping of the birds kept going and the scene around wore a dark look. All was quiet, very quiet, no flap, no flutter, sounds of the dead leaving a hiss and those waiting for the death seemed in no discomfiture. The night appeared round the corner but the evening itself told enormously about the kind of night it was to be. When a hiss falls, the dread rises, the fear shrivels to grovel, the faith disintegrates alarmingly just about everything. The aircraft swings like a pair of wings of a bird flying at an intimidating height, the silence speaking its own language, the occasional movements of the Air Hostesses, the fatigued passengers rocking to the chairs, the arms hanging down, the toilet at the receiving end and the crew blaring from time to time to interfere with the fractured naps of the passengers. Nothing called for a moment's solace from the invisible chaos. It was another two hours, still to remain in the air hung between the air and the land, between the sea and the sky, between the shades of falling grace and fleeing impasse, life seemed a long tail and the aircraft's discordant clamour continued the cajoling affair. Kids, many of them, though resigned to half baked sleep, still were more than restless, mothers pulling their outstretched hands and legs back to the position, grown up girls were not too mindful of their positions. Some had switched on the headlights engaged in flipping through the pages of whatever it might be, some still stayed sterile, incapable of exhibiting anything while asking for water at regular intervals. The oldies seemed fatigued; faces sunk in bewilderment spoke about their dislike of the existing conditions. The high and long stretches of clouds, the aircraft continued piercing through, and some still wandered their dilated eyes to let them stay on the parts of the bodies that were left exposed in a state of unwanted sleep.

The aircraft was on a high altitude, and looked as if it would leave nothing to conquer, rising to conquer but the abrupt fall from the height, jostles all sleeping, momentarily pushing them back from the quasi sleep and reminding them that sleep is not something they can latch on to comfortably. In the midst of all these the cry of a baby would tend to be a volcano and the mother and the baby both would be overactive to sneak into the existing calm. The take off from Delhi was delayed by the fog by three hours. All passengers were already harried before being on board and further seven hours on the trot appeared like a phase in time. Back in Delhi, the weather was inclement; rains falling perpetually, clouds hovered around the sky to keep away the bustling sounds of the Aircraft and the crew praying hard for the conditions to persist. But finally the Airport Authorities decided to fly the Aircraft for the destination. All seemed gay for a moment and the boarding was well on course. It was a huge Aircraft of about three hundred capacity, Royal Jordan, bound for Libya via Amman, Jordan. From Delhi to Jordan were four hours and the transit of about three at the Amman Airport only frightened the passengers. International journey is like a scary long night, where the bundles of clouds are rolled in fearful basket and unleashed through heavy drops of rain. The man behind my seat, coughed and coughed vigorously, would stretch his legs to crash the back of my seat and I would grimace in irritation barely managing a look back blocked by my own seat. Next to me was, a youthful girl, barely in her twenties, eyes were sharp and hazel, a devious nose, lips were cunningly crafted as if it were created by a cunning sculptor, hair, a blend of the black and brown and the build was aesthetic. She wore a sleeveless frock, a short frock, and her three fourth trousers hardly covered her shin. She looked splendid or the impression seemed so, but she was indeed a creature to be with. I thanked heavens that those four hours would be like sitting with the gift of Nature, to be with the grace of a Goddess whom I adored without speaking a single word. I did not speak for the silence between us spoke more than I could have. Sometimes she would lean back brushing my shoulders, and a gale of fresh air rumbled across. The Aircraft's sudden jolt made her a bit skeptical, will immediately cling to the glass of the window as if probing the reason for the jolt and then would look rather disinterestedly towards me, waiting to be seen, to be looked at and to be told something but she never did the last part. In a way I was uncomfortable, for I wanted to lay back without disturbing her, changed position without her knowledge, turned around without letting her feel it but every time I did it , She acknowledged it through gestures only. The body odour permeated my nostrils umpteen occasions and I enjoyed the same with a breathless breath.

For the most part of the flight, it was a hide and seek for me, a game played with utter caution. I went on to become a curious observer, a traveller with an inquisitive mind, a passenger with a working imagination and a reader of the situation with open eyes. To my left was another woman of about thirty-five. A good build, stout in constitution, eyes so wide that the sea can be sunk into it, the eyelashes marked with dark pencil, a husky face and a bemusing smile. I created occasions to look at her and she appealed me hugely and to the extent that I would love to fall in her lap. My heart wandered from one woman to another, eyes travelled widely and alarmingly, scanning the beauty of Nature, perhaps the beauty that dwindles to physical grace, just a physical grace. She perhaps was a little more conscious, perhaps loved gazes reminding her of her prized possessions. But every time I created space to turn around a bit to see her, the note of dissent was lodged by the girl next to me symbolically. I was pretty young, so I thought there to catch the young hearts fancy, to move into the corridors of stray and chanced encounters and in the last two hours I and she had struck a rapport, a solid unspoken rapport with tender, deliberate touches of ignorance. She was rising in confidence, and I could notice the hesitant yet assertive looks enough to suggest the tale graduating into beliefs. The woman left to me was distinctly self conscious, waiting for gazes from all eligible but the tragedy of the situation came to the fore in the form of the elderly presence around her. The man sitting next to her must be in his late fifties with a huge bulk. Pot bellied, a huge structure as if he was asked to block the whole street in the air, encroached her seat to the objectionable extent. But the man was helpless with his bulk. I saw him pushing himself close to her using his bulk for in it he had a ruse and the woman could do nothing possibly.

Every second hour I used to leave my chair to ease myself for the air conditioner had turned the Aircraft into a pack of ice and everybody seemed rolled like a football, shrunk and tapered. Well on way to the lavatory, I would make some ruses to stand right before the woman to my left and while lumbering to the way to the lavatory, I would take as much time as I could possibly to leave me satisfied with her and her looks. I should ideally believe that she wasted no time in letting her be seen by those whom she wanted. But the girl next to me was now beginning to be more assertive in her gestures as I feigned to sleep producing muffled sounds from the depth of the throat, partly to draw her attention and partly to create some moments of irritation. I waited with closed eyes to gauge her reaction to the artificial sounds of my snoring but she used my pretension effectively. She raised her right hand and let it fall and rest on my left shoulder, then she pulled her blanket down and lifted her leg to the possible extent in that congested area, and she looked inside her own frock, in such a way as to make things fairly accessible to the waiting eyes. I turned myself into a statue, even the breath was held hostage for a while only to be broken by a very subdued excuse me, I kept my position intact waiting for the words excuse me to be repeated with the same delicacy. Excuse me sir, the pitch was louder, I acted as if I was in the throes of deep sleep. I am so sorry; I completed the sentence while making way for her. She darted into my eyes, but they were not bloodshot, the eyes seemed drunk with all a man can see with careless deliberation. She moved away but did put her right hand firmly on my shoulders.

While she moved, I felt a gale of fresh air muscling its way to the whole body.

The Aircraft kept oscillating between high and low and the occasional information from the crew members kept pouring in regarding the heights, altitude, wind velocity and the distance left. I stood my ground, visibly broken for legs were folded like a cheap airbag that crumbles even under the lightweight and back was getting stiff. The youthful girl also showed signs of fatigue, turned to me and left a question. Can you tell me the time left for Amman? I did not know whether to say any amount of time or look at the watch and suggest a time. But I had to keep her engaged with her solitary question. I think still we have some time left because I could see the Airhostess still serving water, juices and tea to the request of the passengers and there was no sense of urgency or at least it seemed to be so. I told her to be patient to which she just yawned and closed her eyes. I wanted to initiate the process of conversation for I was getting restless and hated sitting like a dumb driven cattle. But I had no choice. I had to be like that and just looking around. One of the Airhostesses made a very pleasing appearance. Her face was round, wafer thin lips, moved swiftly with long strides and oozed an air confidence about her movements. Her smile made all fall for her. Even her half smile was quite a temptation. White complexioned with a dot like mole on the lower lip made a splendid background and added the element of charisma to her charming self. She walked in beauty with controlled and measured steps to leave hearts thumping. I thought why God grants all to one, to one individual with all precision. The four hours flight went on to become quite a day in history, if not a day then surely a passage in history. Amman was not too far away as came the announcement to fasten the seat belt and push the seat up. The girl next to me hurriedly fastened the belt and looked towards me to check whether I have done it. I did it as fast as she did. The passengers on board showed a lot of urgency in getting the things done and the landing orders were finally given to the crew. The captain announced both in Arabic and English and the dice were spruced up for the landing. I could see through the glass along with the girl the ground beneath laden with patches of grass, hard surface of concrete and the bright sunshine now sneaking into us through the glass pane. The girl looked towards me with words stuck up in her throat but gave me a solid, hard touch with lovely brushes all around my parts. I thought I won her without speaking to her and she thought she overpowered me with her at times hard looks and at times delicate, mild, and even voluptuous looks. She was beautiful, she was all grace Nature infested her and she said the unspeakable through her body language. As the flight landed on the hard concrete runway with a thud, she bumped into me with a sorry.

We came out of the Aircraft together, walking hand in hand only to bid a tearful permanent bye to each other.

# Heavenly Benediction

Kusum's dull pulsing of blood interfered with a sense of ennui creeping into a body that wanted rest after a week's hectic work. However, the same weekend so badly required and waited from the day a new week starts turns out to be a damp squib. Kusum, in the daily business has normally no time to brood over what happened to her and to think who is responsible for whatever she is today. Some of the unresolved contradictions and the dynamics of a tormented existence had trained her into accepting everything without grimacing an inch. She was a cool customer with insurmountable patience. She looked at everything casually, never attempted to see beyond the visible and perhaps this is why she does not embroil herself into the charade of a seeping life. Early childhood is a saga of unpalatable songs and to go back to them is like revisiting the wounds it inflicted on the body and soul of a struggling individual. She looked the other way to drift away from the teeming thoughts and fixed her eyes to the huge hoarding that said," **Be your own and be within**". It appealed to her though she did not get the idea as what possibly it suggested but she thought it sounds good and at night, perhaps she will get back to working it out in terms of a possible connection to life. She hurried her steps back to the house, where she was presently dwelling. Not very far from the office, situated right into middle of a bustling colony where everyday had she met some new people with new tales. She did not know much about these people save a formal hello and bye. She was living alone, not for the first time though she had been with people also but still she was alone. She was all alone in this wide and huge circus of life.

By 8 O' clock she put her first step into the house. Things lay scattered all over the bed. She does not have much time in the morning to put things back in order for she has to run to the office and even if she is late by five minutes she has to pay a price for it. That was life for her. She has been combating the odds with her limited intelligence, common sense and wisdom. She went into the kitchen first, cups of used tea, some filled half with leftover tea, a few pieces of bread that too rat eaten, lying over the ground, sink had a few unwashed utensils. My God, she thought, now she has to do it all. The fatigue of office and an out of order house left no energy within her but she had no choice. She needed an urgent cup of tea. Nothing was in place. Why she does it? She does not know how to find time for all these early morning. Perhaps if she leaves bed early then she might help herself a bit to deal with this clumsy situation. Nevertheless, rising early has never been easy for her. She changed and again walked into the kitchen. As she moved there, her cell chased her with a ring. Oh, no. Who is this? She ran back to her room to check the call. Kusum, the voice from the other side was not very soothing. It was her boss. Kusum. Yes sir. Kusum, you were supposed to see me before leaving office. I had left a word with the secretary. Did she tell you? No sir nothing was said to me by her. Ok. All right. You must report early tomorrow, as we have to prepare a report urgently. Ok. Bye for now. Kusum's plan to do things early in the morning went for a toss. Normally she has to leave around 7 O' clock but tomorrow as the boss says, has to be earlier than that. She wondered as why the secretary did not tell her about it. This secretary is very close to the boss and there are tales that Kusum has been told by some of her colleagues but her reaction is the same. What she has to do with all. She is doing her job and that is all. She again walked into the kitchen to make tea and something for the dinner. Lunch she takes very light and to be hungry is only natural for her by the time she comes back home. Sometimes she takes parcel also but this night she did not feel like going there and thus, she has to cook. No problem, she thought. There are bread and some eggs. She will have it in her dinner and the morning has the fixed menu. Bread and jam. After the dinner was over, she came back to her bed and recalled what she had seen on the hoarding reading, "be your own and be within". She was trying to get to the actual meaning that this entailed. She knew what is to be your own like discovering the self or being within the means or being sympathetic to the limitations one has. May be, may be, she thought she has it right. The other part be within has a reference to one's idea of the self and to know what one can really be good at or about. She relapsed rather hesitantly to the early days of her life, losing parents, almost being a chanced child thrown at the mercy of the philanthropists or the charitable houses. Her remote maternal uncle at Bhilwara picked her up. He took her there as he volunteered to play the guardian of an abandoned child. She was 12 only. That was the beginning of a tormented childhood. Having lost parents in a car accident and being left to fend for herself, she was perched on the dicey podium of life. Her maternal uncle seemed to be a man of fine deportments, elegant habits and a very good looking, a kind-hearted man. Obviously picking up an abandoned child is only through a deep humanitarian concern and she thought; now her woes are over. She happily went to her maternal uncle. For the first six months, she found herself placed comfortably. She was admitted to a good convent and all possible care was there. The wife of his maternal uncle was an ultra modern person and her dress at times surprised her for she had not seen anything like that in her own house. Her parents were orthodox, values loving people and they wore only traditional dresses. She found her dressed scantily at home, just a lose top and Bermuda. While going out she changed into a more pathetic looking woman. She wore a top that exposed her cleavage and a short trouser that went up to her knee only. Heavily painted lips with red blood lipstick, eyelashes and all cosmetics were there in abundance. She would go to parties, clubs and cinema regularly. Her husband was just an orderly for her and there he had no choice.

One fine morning, that was a holiday and her maternal uncle stayed back home while his wife left very early in the morning. She sat alone in her room, perhaps thinking of how things have changed in her life. It was very quiet. She saw her maternal uncle coming twice, thrice towards her room and turning away from there. He seemed restless. She thought perhaps he is not well. She came out, lunged towards his room and asked whether he needed anything. Her maternal uncle was there in his room, as he saw her coming towards him, he just stood and lovingly called her Kusum. Yes uncle. Anything wrong. Do you want anything? No, no, you just come here and sit. There was silence and his uncle had the newspaper in his hand. He at once opened it, pulled her a little closer, and asked her to read a news item. Kusum was nervous. She thought, he never did like this and today he is looking something different. She kneeled a bit, to read the suggested news item and the moment she threw her eyes about the paper, she felt the movement of some fingers running about the lower part of her waist. Initially she ignored it. There was a repeat of the action in no time. She looked at her uncle raising a few questions through her eyes. His uncle looked the other way and insisted on reading the same news item. She did it again. His uncle moved out of the room and re-emerged immediately. He was somewhat uncomfortable. Kusum thought what exactly is he trying to do. Still she was a kid of about thirteen years but her looks suggested much more than that. Her uncle left his position, picked her up and banged her on the bed. He frantically with a sense of urgency forced her blouse up.Kusum was like a defenseless soldier. Her tiny breasts were smooched mercilessly with a pair of hefty hands, her almost invisible nipples were put into the waiting mouth and the hands once freed from the breast ripped the trouser cord. Her clothes were taken off. She was all bare. A pair of tiny boobs hanging down, her thighs bare shone in the diminishing light of the lamp, her armpits were growing, her cunt felt the movement of the fingers running about it followed by the tongue that darted inside to leave some watery stuff. He did not ride upon her. That was the only thing he did not do. He left her in the same position and moved out of the room. She regrouped herself; put the clothes back on the body and in a traumatic state came back to her room and closed the door. The fancy of a growing girl was struggling to come to terms with what happened. She remained in her room, having been ripped and assaulted by her maternal uncle, she had nothing to think. After a few hours, the knock at the door brought her back to life. She opened the door. Her maternal uncle was there right before her. He appeared a normal man smiling and asking whether she has eaten anything. She did not feel like. A short answer did not satisfy her uncle. No, no please you must eat something. He took her by hand, and strode again to his own room. There was a packet of food. He made her eat with lots of persuasion. He also ate with her. Not a word was said about what he did to her. Kusum had no choice but to endure the pain it inflicted and the words of protest she did not know. That was just the beginning of a tale repeated with religious zeal. She did not tell anything to her Aunty, rather wanted to investigate the psyche of her maternal uncle.

Much later after she ran away from there at the age of 16 that she could discover her Aunt's illicit liaisoning with a host of men and her Uncle was a hapless individual tamed so badly by the aggression of a modern woman who found no fault in sleeping with others. She ran away from there badly bruised sexually, physically marred, she was just an object of sexual fantasy for her Uncle. Today she is 22, alone but she does not have the fear to be ripped, to be abused sexually and if at all it happens it will not be a forced one. When she slept, she did not know and when she opened her eyes, it was 6.30 in the morning. She got up hurriedly, took bath and ran to the office, as the boss required her early that day. At office her boss was seated comfortably in his chair, well dressed, humming a tune, which he could listen to himself. The secretary just outside the chamber of the boss cleared her; she barged in hesitantly anticipating a set of instructions that she will have to comply. Sit down young woman, the informal tinge was more than evident. She took her seat and looked on the way a soldier waits for the command from the General. Tea, Coffee. Anything? No. Thank you. Come on no formalities. Kusum was surprised at the informal ways of her boss. She looked into his eyes and there was nothing fearful for her in those eyes. She had not seen him much except occasional calls from him and the calls were so short that she never had the time to have a detailed look at him. He seemed to be a man of taste, elegance and the aesthetics were all personified. Tall, eyes a bit brownish, a wide forehead, well combed hair almost hanging and wavering suggested the portrait of a man who could have impressed anybody's infancy. She shirked her head and got back to the moment. Kusum, I think I have something important to tell you and remember today you will do all these at your home and not here for you need concentration. He whisked out an envelope from the pocket of his coat, handed it over to her and said flippantly, all instructions are there and I want the result tomorrow or may be this evening also. I want immediate result whether you can do it or not. Kusum took the envelope and stood to leave. Good luck young woman, there was grace in his voice. She left the office and put herself on the road back home. Throughout the short distance she was negotiating from the office to her home, she was inquisitive as to the envelope that left her thinking since the time she took it from him. At home, she was in a devil of a hurry to scan the envelope. She threw her vanity bag on the bed and herself and hurriedly opened the envelope with a beating heart and the envelope read.

Kusum.

I was contemplating to have some discussions with you on an issue that merits urgent attention and for the last two weeks I was in a fix whether to tell you directly or should there be an indirect way to tell you what I wanted to. I did not know that. I procrastinated it, suspended it as I was struggling to find a way to communicate something important. However, I was unsure of myself and the kind of reactions it would elicit from you but this letter perhaps will serve the purpose effectively. I have been observing you for quite sometime without letting you know that you are under a scanner. Yes, I did the intelligence and I am guilty of it. Nevertheless, I must confess that there are still people despite stricken by the odds of life look straight, value honesty and commitment. You have stayed focused, and there have been no distractions. I know what you been through early on in life and how it left you reeling. However, your belief in the self, in the goodness of the self saved you from a vertical split. Thank you are the same ebullient self and keep up a bright face. I have had relations with many women in life to tell you very honestly but all of them were money seekers, devoid of any sense of value and a complete wretched. I have seen them how they hammer and hew a formula of sucking wallet. I can only hope to find somebody like you or you if you agree to be engaged in a conjugal relationship. If you have reservations, I would consider myself distinctly unfortunate. I may be excused for going overboard. Please give it a thought and let me know the final verdict.

Thanks. Manudeep Rathore.

Kusum looked at the heavens many a time and heaved a sigh of relief. She thought He does things his own way.

# Root's Cry

Reaching the midway mark, Aftab thought there will be no more ruptures and uncertainties about a life that seemed to have outlived its capacity to embrace anything new. Settled to a decent job, settled to a life that fetched just about the kind of result he would have thought would be there. His life was a bundle of jerks, the unseen blues enveloped it time and again and the pattern that emerged out of it was the one very predictable. From the early days, from the toddling days, from the days of lengthening shadows, his life kept running like a machine that sometimes developed a technical snag and ceased to function for a brief period and that was also a period of the lull before the volcanic eruptions on fronts he never imagined would stretch him to the full. All these crept into the fold of life and he just went along the lines assuming it to be its songs and perils. That was that.

Aftab was not the one with the brightest of minds around nor was he given the kind of exposure to the institutions early on in life that could have done away with the mediocrity tag. He thought, he was the one ordained to be ordinary, commonplace and will have to share the dais with the chosen and celebrated mediocre all through the life but little did he seem to realize that every mediocrity has the unseen spark that on its day can even belittle the genius. His early childhood was spent under the galloping sounds of the greenwood tree, under the shades of the much valued human caresses and under the watchful eyes of those raising him. He was strange in the sense that his mind was the most unstable thing for him for it never entertained any lofty thought or anything magnificent for he seemed resigned to the limitations that set in rather inadvertently. He had a taste for literature without any likes for music. He read books, serious books, and serious poetry, everything serious as though comic interlude did not have any authentic space in his life. He giggled with friends but his heart was never a party to it, he ran on the famished roads of life, on the deserted islands of gloom, walked the cracked and bumpy streets without any song and dance and took things in stride without grudges. Aftab was a solitary player in the game of submission to the odds of life, a character around whom was cast the inevitable drudgery of being.

The monsoon was eagerly awaited as the summer heat sapped all vitality from the bodies of the young and the old. The sun that blazed the earth had the fire to burn even the stubborn of bones and the sky above the head rained down torrents of heat and the wind that blew further intimidated a bewildered creature looking towards the sky for redemption. Aftab, looked at the sky oozing all fire, turned towards the pond that dried up furiously and lumbered down to the rivulet to find it even more crying for a single drop of rain. Drought loomed large and the farmers were committing suicides and those who did not, were in for huge troubles ahead. Hunger, starvation, famine all seemed round the corner. That was the fiercest summer Aftab had seen in his life though he was only twenty two. He was told by his father that in the year 1936, there was a death like scene and the famine only consumed human lives mercilessly. He had been to his native village and there only he saw and experienced what life possibly could be in the absence of modern civic amenities. His mother was upset and did not want him to go there during that period for she thought, her son might be infected with those things she had heard are frequent in villages but Aftab just did not mind visiting his native village. As he put first step forward on the holy land of his native village, he encountered strange scenes, scenes that amused him initially but those were the scenes that left some very deep impressions on him, impressions that he carried with him throughout his life, he reckoned. A blistering summer afternoon, mercury shooting alarmingly, people scantily clad, bare bodied, even women covering bare minimum, kids had nothing on, and they were on the ground, on the floor fanning themselves with handmade fans, with hard clothes, with everything they found handy. Aftab, stood on the edge of the road, inched towards the mound, climbed on it and sat there in the scorching sun to feel the impact of heat on a human body and thereby try and connect it to the people who are facing it as a matter of routine. He had seen the same village Bidhupur, hundred times to say the least but the village had never been so hot, so furious, the temperature just burnt about everything. He thought he just might become a tamasha as soon he thought it, quickly came down and put himself on the road to his home there. He was drenched to the skin, sweat had enveloped his face and the drops of it dripped to the other parts of the body. He finally got into the house much to the surprise of all those present there. People with all that they had entertained him. His grandmother was going mad, howling at people for everything required for him and everybody was pressed into service. Aftab, filled with the warmth of hospitality, with overflowing love of his granny, with the affection showered on him by everybody and the afternoon though it was hot as hell seemed to lose much of its heat under the affection of the people there. The hand fans were in motion under the watchful eyes of granny and if one hand was tired, the alternative was readily provided by granny who would ensure the continued movement of the hand. Aftab felt some fatigue creeping into him and he told the people around to be quiet for he was just gearing up for the nap. Granny thundered with the might of her voice and imposed a veritable curfew on the movements and only those were allowed who could move their hands. Aftab slept and slept well, and it was the nap induced by the tender affection of some very innocent people.

He woke up around five O' clock in the evening to find his granny, squatting on the jaanamaaz waiting for Azan. Aftab crawled towards her and looked into her eyes. She appeared like an angel on earth who has nothing to repent, nothing to brood, nothing to clamour for. Resigned to God at the age of eighty-five with all body parts well in shape that is to say the health issues were not that alarming. She could move on her own, do her things; the voice was not as lifeless as it might have been at that age. Aftab was pleased to see all this and thanked God for everything. It was time for tea and by that time Aftab had started smoking also and it was indeed a problem there to smoke for he did not want his granny to know it. Tea was served by the maid. Granny had many maids at her disposal for her two sons sent her enough money that she could afford a comfortable life. Her maids were hers in the sense that she was a woman who cared for everybody and loved them as her own kids. Aftab, moved away from there to out house that was well within the same campus. He was joined by his cousin but Aftab thought since the moment he landed, there has been nothing from somebody he wanted to be the first person and honestly much of the heat was endured by him for the heck of an individual. Sara did not come and Aftab thought she might be waiting for him. He lunged forward and found his steps on way to Sara.

That was a small village with lots of greenery thrown around. The wide sprawling paddy field, the rough stretches of human steps, the puff of dust produced from every single step, the popularly known "well", as sacred as the "woman" and every single drop of water fetched from it would suffice to purge whatever the vice or affliction was, the popular refrain blinded all faiths. The narrow road, congested as ever and reeling with the loads much the same way as an old man would quip, the road is longer than I and perhaps older than my father also went for years together. Aftab was a child who grew up with such scintillating tales having seen people come from far off places and seek succour in the grace of the "Holy woman" who would not disappoint anybody. Aftab though cynical would go to the well, examine the colour of the water of the well and taste it using his own hands by clubbing them together and depositing them on the clubbed palm to suck the water from the "Health Well" He would generally make some face and then turning towards those present would say humorously, well, this well now will protect me from all unfair advances. The people around would smile and the women would look at each other and try and know something about this child. Those were the better days for him as he moved from the dusty lanes to the by lanes, from the Jamun tree to the Tamarind and from the Tamarind to the orchard of Mahmood Mian. This was the best moment for Aftab, shared by Chamoo Bhai, the master of all that was childish and yet cunning. Can I go back to the event when Mahmood Mian was all asleep in his charpai outside his orchard and came Chamoo Bhai with his battalion only to pick Mahmood Bhai's charpai with incense sticks glowing beautifully and Chamoo Bhai would lift the charpai with his battalion ranting all the way to the graveyard "inna lillahai rajauoon. Mahmood Bhai would keep his legs stretched until the incense stick's aroma would pierce through his stuffed nostrils to disturb him from his sleep and having seen himself being transported to the graveyard in his life only would start heaping choicest abuses on Chamoo Bhai. Once the Chamoo battalion realized that Mahmood Bhai is inching back to life, they would throw the cot along with Mahmood Cha comfortably ensconced in it. Then only Mahmood Bhai, who was old and fiery, would come running to Chamoo Bhai's mother and warn her of dire consequences if her son did not mend his ways. The following day the same story as nothing would deter Chamoo Bhai from his adventurous journey and Mahmood Cha was an easy prey for him. Aftab would see all these and find the humour of life occupying some space in that orchard of the afternoon.

Chamoo Bhai, as he was widely known and called by all, whether young and old for he was the only trouble the village had. He would normally torment the old, the established masters of the village, the emperors of the afternoon and the sleeping dogs outside the orchard. In those tiny advances of Chamoo Bhai, there was the real essence of life as he would be begging apologies of those in the evening whom he tormented during the day. Chachha, for everybody, whether it was Mahmood Mian, Jabban Bhai, Cheque, Ahmadi Mian, Shakoor Mian, Heqroo Mian, Sahabjaan Mian, Shaljam Bhai, Thoor Kattu, (Wasi Mian) Chamoo Bhai spared none and used all his tricks to regale the village by tormenting a few. Normally the life at Bhidupur offered much to think about and Aftab found regaled to the best of his satisfaction and wondered at the same time that life at times can be beautiful and livable too. The relations were wonderful in the sense that poverty celebrated life being independent of the tomorrows and they lived every moment of today's life. May be that was casual, a bit unsavory but they didn't mind that all the same. From the backwaters of the village to the glossy lanes of the city Aftab, found it uneasy though temporarily he allowed himself to be overawed by the imposing rural splendour with a resigned attitude. The early days of life suggest the pattern of the movement, the inclination to hold on to a particular bent of mind or thought or the will to see the days to come later all were irrelevant to Aftab for he was not the kind for whom the happiness of life could be brought back in a single day. For a grudging individual life becomes more difficult and there has to be a good reason to find the semblance of an order in a life that remains in the gripping throes of contradictions. Aftab while trundling through the paddy fields would goad his fancy to rise above the self prejudice and try and see the outside world with the same urgency he would examine his profile. Chamoo Bhai was the one who lived his life in the cynicism of the self and perhaps that was the illusion he escaped into to ward off what was apparent. Chamoo Bhai indeed sung the songs of life without ever bothering to understand what the songs of life exactly were. Soon he shifted to Bangladesh as his father was there and the elder brother known for his glib talking and the imposing lengths of his talks normally scared people away but he was a decent man who was still facing the rough end of the stick. Poverty took Chamoo Bhai away from Aftab as his exodus to Bangladesh left Bhidupur to his fate and the likes of Mahmood Bhai, Shakoor Mian and Heqroo Mian heaved a sigh of relief. But deep down they knew that life at Bhidupur would never be the same again and the vigilance by Mehmood Mian outside his orchard at noon held no dangers and this complacency made him lose his sleep. The village was quiet, Chamoo Bhai had left and Aftab bade a tearful adieu to the jumping Jack of the village and the whole village for a little while found itself stricken by an untold misery. Since then the village remains stripped of its zest for life. That was the moment perhaps much savoured and equally castigated by the denizens of the small village. Aftab wanted to erase everything from the memory that reminded of the vibrant currents Chamoo Bhai represented and the live wire of a village was condemned to its monotony. Chamoo Bhai left plunging the village into an uneasy calm and the hundred years of solitude began from there. Altaf was a little boy at the time Chamoo Bhai left for his envisaged destination but the same Chamoo Bhai had left what possibly went on to become the scars of a lost childhood. Since then Altaf never went back to the days of the childhood only to stay disconnected from the roots, a desire born out of the concern to remain firmly entrenched into the roots.

Later Aftab was told, yes, years later that Chamoo Bhai in Bangladesh didn't find anything of the kind he wanted. That was 1972 perhaps and the country Bangladesh was not a quiet place or rather it has been so from the day it was delivered from subordination. There the Biharis, a good chunk of population that had migrated from India to Bangladesh were not only being targeted but the drive was on to uproot them calling them the outsiders, the immigrants and the Mohajirs. Chamoo Bhai was also a Mohajir refused space in a strife torn country and the insurgency kept escalating. Those that had migrated to Bangladesh in pursuit of livelihood and to find a stable tomorrow were ruing their decisions and the life was under constant threat. The Bihari backlash began and it was a fiercest one known in the human history. Cries of wail, bleeding human bodies, random bullets tossed up in the year, the goons, marauders, lumpens and the hired killers went on the rampage. Humanity was once again stripped of its clothe. Barbarism knew no limits and a veritable bedlam were created. Aftab had nothing to do with what was happening in Bangladesh or happening to it save the fact that the little heart was bleeding for his pal, the jumping Jack, the one who kept injecting life into a morose village. Later on, when all seemed lost and his mother a tormented lady had stayed back in the village to wait for the rehabilitation of the three, the two sons and a father but little did the woman realize that she was waiting for the impossible. Hannan Bhai, the much revered character, the ever ebullient, the unfazed master of the human destiny was consumed by the sectarian violence in Bangladesh and the very dear Chamoo Bhai fell apart, lost and disappeared in the stream of the running time. The dream land turned into a savage land and the hopes were crashed to the graveyard. Bangladesh became the land of the marauders, of the aggressors, of the perpetrators and the killers of the crawling human breath. In the sectarian upheaval the Bihari's were left high and dry and the escape route was not coming forth. The elder brother returned to India having lost the father and the brother, Chamoo Bhai, disappeared mysteriously. He was left to fend for himself and the ailing mother who did not break into hysterical sobs as tragedy was an inalienable part of her life. She reconciled to the loss of the son and the husband without making any bones. Her bones had dried up, she did not have the courage to wail nor did she have the intent to beat her chest. She was indeed a very consolable character and stood convinced of the struggle ahead. Struggle was the principle of her life for she refused all handshakes with the giggles of life. Doman Bhai, returned to embrace the lost roots, to rediscover his past, to try and find a responsive chord in the same village that was disowned by his father. The call was more emotive than ever and the reconciliation was more dramatic than the sojourn to Bangladesh. Soon the same

Bangladesh assumed menacing forms for him for it was there only that he wanted to eke a living and in turn he compromised with the loss of the brother and the death of the father. The old lady with the growing wrinkles thwarted with courage the catastrophic aftermath of whatever she went through and in it she saw the flickering flame still willing to gnaw it down to the wicks. Doman Bhai wanted to start his life afresh discarding all disturbing memories behind him. Aftab remembers vividly how Doman Bhai came to Gaya to meet my father and the two wept for hours together. Aftab consigned to a remote corner was very observant and could see the union between the two and in the same union he found the roots being discovered and the drops of tears rolling down the cheeks told a sordid saga of disintegration of the souls only. Doman Bhai had almost turned into a jackpot almost suffering a mental disbalance only to suggest the impact of the tragedy that he could not endure. Now the issue before him was that of reconciliation after the destructions suffered and endured by him and the visit recalls Aftab, was to find some wherewithal to rebuild his life from the ruins. It was not easy as he was bereft of all resources and seeking things from people in a family that was still busy building its fortune. Aftab's father did whatever he could and promised further to do his bit in helping him to reorganize himself. Doman Bhai was all broken and the rebuilding was not that easy, he realized the indifferent world though this indifference of the world was nothing new for him. He was more than a man having seen the rough edges, the tough roads leading ahead and the dimmed light of a life refusing to find any meaningful way to re-assert the clumsy and falling saga. Doman Bhai soon found the road ahead too bumpy and went back to the village to give himself some breathing space before he could regroup himself. All seemed to fall apart and he was a mute spectator.

Aftab enjoyed every bit of his stay there and while leaving the village a drop of tear gushed up into his eyes and he wiped it out with a resolution that he will stay connected to his roots, to the same roots that were under a realistic threat of liquidation. He remembered just about everything including Sara who waved her hands, looked pale and lost and in the act of waving her hands she communicated everything she wanted to say. He recalled all details, his days there, and the adventures with Chamoo Bhai, the spirited afternoons, the moonlit nights, the holding of hands with Sara on the terrace. The nights were sparkling for the light, the moon heaped on earth was golden and he revelled in those golden moments. Today when he looks back, he finds it is hazy, it has the tinge of pain, and it has the flickering memories. Those days, he thought were the days independent of all apprehensions, where the fancy was born without the strain of realism.

# Fantallon Island

The darkness deepened fast, the silence trailed in hail, the evening sunk in confusion, the sky diffident to look in its elements, the dogs and dodges, the clouds and clamours, torches gleaming lights fading away to stall the falling fog. The sea at its fiercest best, the waves crashing into stones and ricocheting to the far end of the same sea, that was more than willing to open up jaws to gulp down its throat the soft and hard, the strong and weak, the loosely structured and solidly built. It was hungry, more than hungry and its tide rose and fell, with diminutive power to annihilate the semblance of life at the sea.

Through the darkest layers of the waves, through the slightest gush of the wind, through the smallest particle, it was customary for sea to find its way and leave things whatever it might be exposed to the dangers of death. Sea is death, the blue water, the depths it has underneath, the sun that falls on the gleaning water finds it more hapless than the clouds that watch it from quite a distance. Roberto Charles Rodrigue, has been a part of the same sea, an inseparable part, a party to the excesses of the sea, has been watching its ferocity, its splendid indifference, its penchant to consume just about everything. His childhood, much of it had seen sea's ability to strike, to unleash terror, to wreak havoc, to play the dangerous game of death, to let the bodies float on the surface. Celina had dived into the sea, the little Charlie, did the same and they were the dives of death. Rosie Jell, Cinthra Balls, Piere Claire, Suzi Hemantha, Larwood Phillips and Jane Hana were the first ones to arrive at the Fantallon Island.

Fantallon island as the myth goes was discovered by the world wide travellers, by the searching imagination of those engaged in geographical expeditions, by the ever so inquisitive human endeavour to strike a responsive chord with the unseen part of the world and by the ones unrelenting in the pursuit to reduce the world to a small village. Roberto Charles Rodrigue, was one such individual to unearth people and places and Fantallon Island was his discovery. Who was he, nobody knows, where did he come from again there is a question mark about it, what exactly he wanted to do, nothing can ever be certain about it. The silence of history, the myths of past, the indifference of time all work in tandem to push the details of Roberto Charles Rodrigue in sheer conundrum. But one thing was certain that he was a human being on a mission, the mission to explore the invisible world, the desire to do something memorable, to be etched in the realms of human memory. The grapevine has it that he was white, obviously from the same race that toppled the world, that mesmerized a good part of the human race and that queered the pitch to advance in the vanguard of science. Roberto Charles Rodrigue hemmed in all myths, stories, fiction to create the splendour of an island today is widely known as Fantallon. He was a globetrotter, a nomadic creature whose feet did not rest until his end and he bounced like a rubber ball to create as much elasticity as would have been possible. He rode the waves of sea, he glided through the rough edges of water, he sailed underneath the depths of sea without being a sailor, without the expertise of a diver, he plunged to the rock bottoms of the mighty sea without fearing sharks and whales, without being aware of his human strength but he sailed and sailed to the final breath. The first human foot that tramped Fantallon was his. Did he find human beings and if the answer is no then who inhabited this? But it is certain that he found the remains of a wrecked ship, the skeletons of human bodies, the bones flung to the far end, the skulls in good measure, and the organs all dried up under the blazing sun and the traces of some life around the same island. But did anybody exist by the time he stumbled upon the island is as much a guesswork today as it has been. But there are signs and symbols that speak of life there at the same island though Roberto was the one who brought it to the knowledge of the world.

Fantallon Island was surrounded by dense forest, with long trees of different hues, plants of obscure nature, insects of the unidentified race, animals of the extraordinary breed, with sea encircling it from all quarters and right in the middle of it were the long intimidating shouts of the sharks that left it more mysterious. It looked like a house under water, a house of glass that makes it translucent. .. But… was there life…..who knows….

Roberto lived amidst all these, was a witness to its mysterious aura, to its glory and grandeur and to its perplexing dynamics. The island was dark, the beauty emanated from its being undisclosed to the outside world. The tumult of the sea, the whizzing sounds of water, the screeching voices of the birds, the howls of the jackals, the galloping sounds of the Winder beasts, the serene yet motivating noises of the butterflies and the captivating yet disturbing quietness of the backdrop impressed Roberto to be into the shrills and thrills of it. When he first arrived on the island, it was desolate, a broken link between the chaos of the inhabited world and the depths of silence of the island. He was astounded over his own discovery, over his own adventurous zeal and his own waywardness culminating into an expedition without the knowledge of science, without the support of technology and without the awareness of its geographical locations. He was an individual lost in the stream of time, involved in exploratory activity. Columbus is widely known for gifting the world with a nation hell-bent upon creating troubles of unseen magnitude to the mankind but Roberto did not discover an island which could be a potential threat to human peace yet nobody knows him. Why…….

Roberto was noble soul who set a goal to himself, the goal to understand the fury of nature and the human inability to prevail upon it. Ahab failed, Santiago was destroyed but Roberto neither failed nor was destroyed. He also took on the might of the whales, of the sharks but did not find Melville or Hemingway to be idealized as hero or his heroism did not fire the imagination of any writer and hence died unsung, unlamented and unreported.

Little Charlie with his sister were sitting on the bank of the sea. It was a dry afternoon and the heat picked up intensity. Both were watching the sea from a distance. Suddenly a roar came about and the velocity of the waves hit them hard but they knew the ways to escape. They ducked in time and let the waves cross over their heads. When the velocity subsided they raised their heads inching closer to the sea that was now friendly. Celina could not resist the temptation of a swim since she knew swimming well and had been doing it quite regularly. Going into the sea held no terrors for her and she swam many times without fear though Larwood Phillips was dead against this adventure of Celina. But Celina had the power of youth and the exuberance of a young mind to ignore the wisdom of experience. She put the first leg forward into the sea, followed by the second, then half of the body well immersed and then the whole of it. She turned upside down, floated on the surface of the water, did a summersault while going to the deep layers of the sea, exerted her hands, swung her legs and in no time she was into the deadly throes of the same sea that does not spare anyone from its uncertain temper. While she was inching closer to the jaws of death, Little Charlie thought his sister is enjoying the swimming and flung himself to the sea to join her under water. Celina could not disengage herself from the mighty clutches of the shark and Little Charlie paid the price for his ignorance of what actually happened to his sister. Both were ready food for the ever famished big fishes. Larwood Phillips could barely do anything to retrieve the parts not liked by underwater rulers. Larwood Phillips was heading the Anthropological Mission undertaken by the Global Anthropological Studies. He lost two kids while pursuing the entrusted duty. Rosie Jell, Piere Claire, Suzi Hamantha, Cinthra Balls and Jane Hana were frightened to the extent that they persuaded Larwood Phillips to abandon the mission but he was a committed man and the personal tragedies did not hinder his goal. He wanted all to be sent back to Columbia but all decided to continue with him though scared and frozen like ice and dead as dry leaves.

Fallaton Island witnessed every day the naked dance of the savage and hugely ferocious sharks and whales and the human fallibility to its dangerous designs. But Larwood Phillips unmindful of the repercussions resolved to find a way to deal with the underwater rulers. He designed a harpoon, made of wood, with a knife attached to the end of the stick that was solid as rock and inflexible as stone. Another weapon that he created for the self defence was a long wooden stick bended from the root that curved and tilted a bit to the left with a huge net fastened towards the end of the stick which he could use effectively against a jumping shark. The idea was to get the neck of the shark entangled into the net and then to roll the stick many a time so that the very neck revolved and cracked eventually. The invention of weapons by Larwood himself sufficed to instill the confidence into him to subdue the vast and enormously dangerous species of Nature. And there began a battle between the techniques of Larwood and the muscle of the whales and sharks.

Larwood gradually turned the sea into a personal enemy and resolved to put up a fight regardless of its strength. Obviously he was hurt, deeply hurt and it was not a case of personal retaliation since it was out of question that he could have coughed up the resources to challenge the sea but he was a human being who had assigned himself a task, a difficult task though not impossible. Fantallon Island, with all its serenity and beauty girded up to witness a classic representation of the human will to transcend the limitations of its own strength. The sun blazed down full throttle, the water glistened like a pot of gold, the sea rose and fell with the tides and the wind blew at a good pace. Larwood stuck to the bank of the sea, took to his haunches, held the harpoon in his right hand and threw the net hemmed in to the top with a knife that was pointed towards the sky anticipating the sharks around the corner. But little did he realize that human element no matter so full of determination cannot wedge a war against nature and the sharks and whales were not ordinary creatures. He put the net into the water, took control of the harpoon, edged closer to the edge of the bank of the sea, put his front leg forward transferring the weight of the body to the hind leg as if he had a gun in his hand and all he needed to do was to press his finger on the trigger. He remained in the same position waiting for the shark to appear for about two hours. Not even a bubble out there in the middle of the sea appeared and eventually Larwood folded up his harpoon but was more than happy that he could at least send a message to the mighty creatures, he could create a sense of warning to them and induce a sense of danger into them. He was gay, humming a tune to the self walked back to the camp. As soon as he came across Rosie Jell, Jane Hana, Piere Claire, he shouted from a distance, I dwarfed them, I dwarfed them, yes, I made them disappear. All three were bemused over the shout of Larwood for they could not understand the logic of his shouts. Jane Hana looked into the wide eyes of Piere Claire as if asking what really was wrong with Larwood.

Cinthra Balls was critically ill for the last few days. Perhaps it was a mosquito bite and she ran high fever. She had turned pale, looked yellow as if the whole blood from the body had switched away. Whatever the medicines that were available were already administered and it made no difference and she continued to reel under fever. Day one, day two and about a week and she deteriorated at a rapid pace. She turned meek, very meek, and there was nothing anybody could have done about it and she in no time lost a whole lot of weight. Larwood, ran frantically across the island, plucked whatever herbs he could find, did all that he could have done within reach but the script for Cinthara Balls was already written while the Anthropological Studies continued and they could collect all evidence of the human existence, the traces of life and whatever Roberto Charles Rodrigue did to unearth the Fantallon Island were well documented but Cinthara Balls had already breathed her last. It was death number three. Larwood progressively turned cynical, found himself placed on a mound of explosives waging a war against the imperious Nature. Larwood in the dead hours of night would stroll down to the bank of the Sea with the same self designed harpoon as his best defence against the rampaging evils of Nature. He put aside the harpoon on the ground, as the darkness gained momentum, the moon above heaped enough light and the shadow of the moon fell into the middle of the sea. Amid all these a graceful silence existed between Larwood and the Sea. A moment's quietness fell. The reflection of his own shadow appeared too long in the water and he was so alert that even a bit of wobble in the sea would have awakened him to the possibility of the dangers. The harpoon was close to his body, he stretched his legs, eyes roved ferociously but a spell of sleep gained currency. He drifted to sleep.

The two lovely kids were running about the island. White faced, laden with exuberance led by the gracious presence of Nature, they kept moving about the periphery of Sea, jumping, dancing, hopping, gay and jocund. The primal smile was a wonderful thing to look at. The kids chased each other, made houses on the sands, took dips in Sea, came out of it and jostled around with fervour and energy. Larwood saw all these, the running kids, the blue water of the Sea, the long jumps of the sharks, the lovely guiles of the dolphins at the bank of the Sea, the hunters being chased away by an unseen fear and he himself taking long dips in the Sea emerging out of it unscathed, unhurt and undefeated. Celina was all smiles, Little Charlie embraced the dolphins and caressed his hands about its body that was huge and firm, hard and rough and still there was tenderness about it. He saw it through the water of the Sea that a young woman called Cinthara Balls is smarting her way through the middle of the Sea, giggling and the drops of water dripping from her body, the drops of water were not ordinary, they were spiritual sprouting from a spiritual body. He saw Cinthara Balls engaged in a dialogue with nature, the dialogue that was about the importance of Sea, its role in the ecological balance, its need to be friendly and furious with those challenging its might. He would see one of the whales talking humbly about the security of the human beings, its honest intention to remain calm even in the wake of provocation but there was no commitment that it would not strike back if human tampered with or intruded into its domain. He also could notice the smiling face of Roberto Charles Rodrigue as if he had been asking about his own discovery with a statement that he was not Columbus.

Larwood was brought back to the reality of Sea by a sudden jolt as if somebody had picked and dropped him from a certain height. As he regrouped himself to come to terms with the situation, there was huge flutter in the sea and the sound was appalling. He immediately took hold of the harpoon, gripped it firmly and sliced through the mounting waves to be at a striking distance from the sharks. As he immersed his front leg into the Sea, he found himself pushed into and almost glided to the far end; he held the harpoon aloft in his right hand being pushed into the depths of the deep Sea, still managing to throw the net with a knife pointed towards the middle of the Sea. He could feel that the net was getting heavy and he thought may be he has succeeded in cramping the shark for space and he started rolling the harpoon in a bid to get the neck of the shark revolved and cracked. There was something red in the water and he was further pleased to find that finally he has been able to strike his tormentor as the shark was bleeding but little did he realize that it was his own blood that turned the water of the Sea red. His one limb was missing and he floated on the surface of the water still latching on to the harpoon and he thought the harpoon was coming handy to him since it became much lighter. The harpoon had lost the knife attached to it at the end of the stick and the tilt that was created to get the neck of the shark was completely damaged. Finally he had a half harpoon in his hand. A broken harpoon was all he could retrieve from the Sea apart from the lost limb.

# Forest Wisdom

Cars sped at dangerous speeds, Geeps of the Khaki clad officers ran on the deserted roads with a sense of disdain. It was black, deep black, the night at its fiercest best, the fire of balls stretching out to the far end of the jungle, charred human bodies getting roasted, grilled flesh littering the roads, the same roads once were the darling of the crowd, the hub of all glamour, the cynosure of all eyes but in just about a week's time It turned into the road of death, the road to disaster and the road to a stigma that spared none of its proud traveller. A long road does not have pauses, does not arrest the flow of thoughts and does not interfere with the chaos of speed. The race was always on; the race independent of all races ran on the long and the wide stretches of the same roads. The darkness threw its tentacles to compound the human cries, to chase the animals straying on to the roads to see what could be more savage than them, more animalistic than their dodgy claws but they hung their heads in shame, utter shame, looked into each-other's eyes as if questioning them to find the limits of bestiality. They had no answers and they decided to take a stroll back into the same den that they thought was a better place to be in for there would be no ripping business, no interference of the human steps, no attacks by the bestial humans and while lumbering down to the forest they kept lamenting the loss of human lives.

The deep and dark patches of darkness falling on the helpless roads and the blood stains sparkled as if there was a sun breaking through the cordon of clouds. The night remained a witness to the screeching sounds of the cars and other heavy vehicles trampled the crushed human bodies. There was no blood in it; there were no flesh on it either for the skeletons of the bodies was without food for months together. The silence that gripped the atmosphere spoke a language replete with disgusting horrors clad in termite. The human beings bestowed with the best of wisdoms, intelligence, senses, civilizational ethos looked towards the animals from the forest to find a clue about compassion, co-existence and the will to be more reasonable in conduct. The lions and tigers who had made on the spot-inspection of the human bestiality convened an urgent meeting to discuss the crisis created by the unmindful and horror infested wars unleashed against its own race. The senior most lion, Gritty, along with his colleagues sat together to take a stock of the gory situation in the human land.

Gritty, in a voice studded with sympathy and pain addressed the collection of individuals in a very sombre mood beginning with a concern to probe human failure to be civilized, to know the limitations of the rights, to argue the fair play in the drama of being and how to remind them that life is lived without encroaching upon the liberties of the individuals of the same society. The constitution of the animal world was referred to as a source to find clues about the holes governing the human society. Gritty began his address with a reference to their own constitution that stated in the Article one of its preamble:-

(A) "All animals are equal. There is no concept of privileges and it will not be determined by the build, class and constitution of the individual animals. All will have the right to tread and trundle about the forest to hunt for food and the hunts made by one will not be encroached upon by the others.

(B) "The lions, tigers, elephants, leopards, hippos, will not use the physical might to dwarf or intimidate the lesser mortals.

(C) The weak and poor will be taken care of by the strong and the powerful. The management of forest will be done by the lions, tigers and elephants with a concern to leave a fair amount of space for the downtrodden and there will be no zones to be known as "no movement zones " by any one.

(D) Leopards and cheetah fairly quick in their movements will not use their speed to terrorize the lesser creatures nor will they do anything to subdue the rights of the weak.

(E) The lions will have the discretionary powers to settle all disputes and the right to elections will not be confined to the upper class only. A rat if it thinks can challenge the lion will be free to do so. All political rights are due to all citizens without prejudice and discrimination.

(F) A body of the powerful animals will look into the grievances of the downtrodden and redress according to the merits of the case.

(G) The horses will be called for some voluntary service in the event of the construction of the houses and will be paid the wages fixed by the financial committee.

(H) There will be no restriction on the intercaste marriages and will be monitored by the appointed committees.

(I) There will be no divide between the urban and rural and the rights to have an equal share in the resources will not be hindered.

(J) If a human being attacks the forest, it will be the collective responsibility of all citizens to fight united.

While the articles of the constitution were being read out by Gritty, his wife, Suzi emerged with snacks and tea for those in the meeting and the meeting took a break with Gritty addressing all saying that there is a core agenda still to be discussed and this will be done after the break. All nodded their heads.

After the break was over, Gritty with his deputy, Slodge, took to the mound and declared from there "Ladies and Gentlemen, today we have a very important issue to discuss and the issue is of urgent importance. We have been living together in complete peace and harmony for years together and there has never been any ethnic or communal trouble ever in the history of this forest of Jaanpur. The Muslims, the Christians and the other minorities have been living with full rights and there was no occasion when their rights were threatened or they ever faced the wrath of the administration. If the life in jungle can be governed with so much of ease and authority and the animals can abide by the rules of the jungle, and then why the human beings whom God has granted with the best of everything can't exist in harmony?" The question was generally applauded by all and the fox, Lucy blinked her eyes while wondering over the problem of the human land and she expressed her ire also that why the animal land is so much concerned about the human land for the same human land has threatened them time and again with their powers and they even wanted to raise colonies over the very land of the forest. The question of

Lucy was not mocked at by Gritty but with a cool mind he asked Lucy to be quiet. It is the demand of the humanity to set things back in order about the human land infested with huge issues of importance as to save the life of one human individual was as much the concern of Gritty as that of the lives of the animals. Lucy nodded her head in agreement and apologized for her interruption. Gritty declared that a representative body of the animals will meet the governors of human land and try and restore the much needed calm. Gritty in the continued breath suggested the names of Lucy, the fox, Admiral, the rat, Bride, the elephant, Muster, the hippos, and from the women folk, he suggested the names of Hanna, the cat, Anna, the deer, Follio, the winder beast and Lizi, the aunt. Gritty fixed the date for 15th August for a meeting with the Prime Minister of the human land. Fidel, Jackal, the secretary to Gritty was asked to send the formal letter of request to the Prime Minister of the human land for the meet. Gritty finally announced the end of the meeting and asked for the necessary preparations to be made on an urgent basis. All the appointed delegates were asked to come in the formal dress in an act of solidarity. All agreed and the meeting was over.

On the 15th of August the delegation of animals led by Gritty marched to the city of Delhi in the national dress to have a formal meeting with the Prime Minister of the Human land. Hanna, the cat was excited to the extent that she walked shoulder to shoulder to Gritty expressing both amusement and the desire to see some of her own race away from the forest as those of her fraternity living in the human land, to know something about their life there though Gritty was serious and was on a mission. Follio, the winder beast, hopped with long steps while Gritty's wife, Suzi moved with Admiral the rat and the two got on well. The delegation reached Delhi and at Vigyan Bhavan they were received by the dignitaries and accorded a warm welcome. Admiral rat, jumped on to the chair and rolled his tongue about the delicacies set on the dining table as the lunch time was just round the corner. Gritty took a serious note of it and chided him to get back to his chair. All the delegates from the forest were introduced to the Prime Minister of the human land. Gritty shook hand with the Prime Minister and they took their respective positions for the all important dialogue. Follio, winder beast, looked serious and time and again he flicked his tongue about his mouth only to be reprimanded by Gritty who meant business. The discussion was initiated by Gritty after the formal greetings. Gritty drew the attention of the Prime Minister to the blood infested riots that recently shook the whole of the human land.

Gritty began with a question that we all are very concerned about the kinds of violence that erupted recently and took the whole human land in its grip while the administration was reduced to a hapless spectator. He pulled a charter of questions from his coat and placed it on the table. We the animals are without knowledge and wisdom, without the common sense, without the mind to think but still we are living in perfect harmony. There is no communal tension even though we have a pluralist society and the religion is diverse. See we are guided by the oral constitution and the constitution acts as the guardian of the forest. We join each other in moments of celebration and distress. We have created a system where the discrimination is not practiced. The weak and the oppressed are given their full rights. The minority is fully protected by the laws, the national resources are equally shared and there is no corruption. We are a democracy where elections are held and full political rights are given to ants also though they are the weakest of the lot. But the human land seems to be in serious trouble. Just a week back there was a blood bath and I and Slodge visited the spots and found human bodies charred, burnt and riddled in a pool of blood while the cars kept running on the road. What is the problem sir and why can't you manage your human land as effectively as we manage.

The Prime Minister of the human land listened with rapt attention and groped for answers. After a moment's pause he began in a defeated voice. Yes, we are humans and we can think. God has gifted us with the best of minds and we are on the rampage with the scientific discoveries, "but still you fight with your fellow citizens and classify and divide citizens in classes and religious segments," interrupted Gritty that unnerved the Prime Minister a bit but still he persisted with his speech. "See, Gritty, We are humans and the problem is the management of the individual ambitions, the rise of fundamentalist politics, the desire to usurp the national wealth by individuals and the imperial hegemony imposed by the west. These problems the forest does not face and your total concern is food." Gritty lost his patience and shot back "though we need food as much as you do but there is no blood bath for it. If we have a piece of bread we share it equally and if you have five pieces of breads you tend to confine them to the selected few and therefore the imbalance." The Prime Minister was clueless and staggered a bit in the chair. Before he could resume, Hanna, the cat went under the chair and touched the thumb of the Prime Minister that made him jump a bit. Gritty again chided Hanna strongly and ordered her to get back to her seat. She obeyed. Slodge, the deputy of Gritty had a question that why is it that the humans are never satisfied and they siphoned off the national wealth. Why there is no accountability for it. The Prime Minister of the human land was finding it difficult to answer the questions and time and again he scratched his head. While the discussions were on Slodge fired another salvo on the Prime Minister. "Why the Muslim minority is not protected here and their political rights are violated. Why they have been the second class citizen though their contribution to the freedom is as much as that of the Hindus? Why there has been a bias against them and very often they are discriminated against?" The barrage of questions unleashed by Gritty and Slodge pushed the Prime Minister on the back foot and he found himself defenceless. Then came the roaring voice of Muster, the hippo, "See Mr. Prime Minister, set things back in order like restoration of the rights of the minorities, a complete check on the genocide for the government is killing the Muslim minority, on the flimsiest of the pretexts calling them terrorists. This is not fair for a democratic country. Is it not?" The Muster hippo sounded fearful and warned the Prime Minister in no uncertain terms. Bride the elephant raised his trunk in anger and told the Prime Minister categorically, "We have Muslims in our community and we have done no injustice to them. We have not decimated their mosques as you did, we have not burnt their houses as you have burnt, we have not outraged the modesty of their women as you have done and what is this all. You have a constitution to go by, you have a political system to be governed by and then and still there are violations." The Prime Minister was cornered on all fronts and all he could do was an assurance that from now on no discrimination will be practiced against anybody and there will be no genocide." And it if happens, again then Gritty, warned the Prime Minister that if at all you repeat the history, then we will have no options but to take over and listen Mr. Prime Minister, this is your last chance to mend ways. The discussion came to an end and the delegation led by Gritty met a cross section of the Muslim populace and assured them of their full co-operation. They all left back for the forest under Gritty.